A self help book on How To Starve your Distractions and Feed your Focus.

YOU ARE THEE PRIORITY

DEVESH SINGH

BlueRose
Publishers

First Published in December 2020

ISBN: 978-93-5427-049-9

BLUEROSE PUBLISHERS

www.bluerosepublishers.com
info@bluerosepublishers.com
+91 8882 898 898

Cover Design:
Jasleen Ashata

Typographic Design:
Ilma Mirza

Distributed by: BlueRose, Amazon, Flipkart, Shopclues

Dedication

This book is dedicated to you. Obviously you. Because You Are The Priority.

And I dedicate all my writings to Shivangi

(The Shiva Soul), that guides me and enlightens me every day.

A special note of thanks to my mom, dad and sisters Harsha and Rashmi Sharma for their constant support.

Acknowledgement

The journey of finding myself and making myself the priority was a significant one and I am thankful to my friends and family who supported me all this time. Even though they already know how much I love them, I take this chance to express my gratitude to them for being through the thick and thin of my life. At the same time, I want to thank my readers who may be going through a darker phase of life, and I want to remind each one of you that there is a light inside each one of you that is waiting to shine and show the path, all you need to do is channel into your energies and remind yourself each day that YOU ARE THEE PRIOIRTY.

Content

Preface

In 1977, two Voyager spacecrafts left our planet to embark on a historic journey to explore the universe. Both of these spacecrafts carry a time capsule which aims to tell a story about Earth and everything in it, to any extraterrestrial life that comes across the spacecrafts. This time capsule is in the form of a phonograph record. The 12-inch gold-plated copper disk known as the Golden Record includes a repertoire of sounds and images collected from all parts of the world to show the diversity of life and culture on our planet.

We have, for a long time, harbored the idea of life beyond our planet and thought of all the ways in which we can extend our presence in the universe. Some think of aliens as our doom while others toy with the idea of friendlies and the inter-planetary exchange of technology.

As Carl Sagan explained, we are only but a pale blue dot in this expansive universe.

So, why is it that our eagerness to explore life beyond Earth has been so high and yet if we were to look at things on a microscopic level, we would realize that as humans we may have failed our own race in terms of compassion and humanity?

According to a 2016 report by WHO, 800,000 people commit suicide every year around the world. At the same time global divorce rates between 1970 and 2008 jumped from 2.6 divorces to 5.5 divorces for every 1000 marriages. And, a millennial and Gen Z survey by Deloitte showed that close to half of the survey respondents, 48% of them, said they were stressed all the time.

These are signs of a society where loneliness, depression, anxiety and stress is an overwhelming problem. Even though mental health awareness is on the rise, our society has moved to a state where loneliness is no longer a choice but a way of life.

When South Korea came into the spotlight for its alarmingly high suicide rates, a lot of organizations studied the patterns to identify the reasons why so many people chose to end their life abruptly. It was found that societal pressure, fear of victimhood, academic performance, and even physical appearance caused several South Koreans to kill themselves. This pattern resonates with suicides in most parts of the world.

The COVID-19 pandemic, jolted the world into another series of problems from battling a seriously dangerous virus to holding up a crumbling economy and working on climate change problems which can cause further disasters affecting thousands of families around the planet.

As the Voyager spacecrafts float away into a universe that we have been eager to explore, back home, on our planet, we are struggling with more problems than before. Many of us accept life as it is and have chosen to walk on the same roads carved out by generations before us.

But the truth is that all of the problems we face today have solutions, workable solutions, which can make all the difference that we have been hoping for. From reviving our biodiversity to reducing the burgeoning problems of depression and anxiety faced by several people in the society, the answer lies in how we see the world and how we see ourselves.

Wake up every morning with the singular thought that 'You Are The Priority'. Be mindful of your actions, your choices and your habits to be kind to yourself, to the planet and to the people around you. This one change leads to a ripple effect bringing about the positivity that you may have been yearning for.

My book covers the nuances of living a gratifying life which puts every single one of you at the center of the love and attention we all deserve and desire.

Introduction

Christmas, 2019 was different than usual for the Norwegian Royal Family which experienced the unexpected loss of Ari Behn, former husband of Princess Martha Louise and father of their three children. In a 2009 interview he had said that he used to be chronically depressed and lonely. The Princess and Ari Behn had divorced in 2017.

For a person of such massive influence and expansive network, many of us may find it difficult to figure out how depression works. Some do not even understand the phase that they may be going through because depression can be difficult to diagnose. Like Ari Behn, we have celebrities, luminaries and even royals who chose to take their lives because of stress, anxiety and depression.

As much as we may all want to colour our lives with the most vibrant and beautiful colours available on a paint palette, we may sometimes find ourselves stuck with the blues and greys when our life throws unproportionally big problems on our way. At other times, it could be lots of small problems that we face in our daily lives which causes us to retract into a shell where we can stay till the time the problems go away. But problems don't just go away.

We have to often fight against them, find a solution to deal with them or simply face them to continue on our journey of life. Because we cannot retrace ourselves into the past and solve the same problems again and again till we get it right, every step that we take should be followed with understanding and acceptance of our actions because we will not have the ability to change what we have already done.

I had a houseplant that I really liked. I took care of it all the time. It flourished well and grew quickly. I was very proud of how beautiful it had grown. But when a big project came my way, work became more demanding. I had less time for other things in life and so my plant started getting lesser time than I had given it earlier. Every now and then I saw a yellow leaf falling down my plant and then I'd remember to water it and care for it. The tips of the leaves started turning brown and slowly, the plant began to die. By the time my project ended, the plant had suffered a lot. I realized how careless I had become not just with my plant but several other things in my life, like my diet, my relationships, my exercise schedule, and the overall quality of my life had degraded. I decided to be more mindful of the things I am doing, and set out on a path of repairing the damages I had caused. My plant started thriving again and so did my life. I continued to expand the horizons for my work and took up bigger projects, but all this time, I was more wary of the quality of life I lived and ensured that my work did not damage my overall life.

When I made these transformations in my life, I realized how the society allows us to believe that successfulness in life comes from compromises at different levels. A large part of the population grows thinking that work-life balance does not exist. A workaholic is often put on pedestal as the ideal employee, and the kind of staff that your office wants. Students with 99% marks are praised all the time and praised so much that everyone else is made to feel like they are not worthy of education. Love between partners is exalted by our society so much that the average couple has a world of expectations from their partner and lots of inadequacies about themselves.

I want you to know that you are the priority. That you deserve the love, the praise and the happiness that you see around and if you feel robbed of any of these emotions, it is important to realize that the ability to transform your life positively lies in you too!

Chapter 1

Finding Reason and Symptoms

Ernest Hemingway was a popular American writer known for best-sellers like *The Sun Also Rises*, *A Farewell to Arms* and the short story *Hills Like Elephants*. He was awarded the Nobel Prize for Literature in 1954. He became an author with an international reputation when his book *Old Man and the Sea* was published. Hemingway won the Pulitzer Prize for fiction in May 1952. He wrote a lot throughout his life and travelled to Paris, Spain, Cuba, and the Caribbean.

In 1960 a news reported that he was seriously ill and that he was on the verge of dying. He wrote a cable to his worried wife Mary that the reports were false and that he was enroute Madrid. The truth was that he really was sick and he often felt so lonely that he would take to his bed for days. Constantly worried about money and safety. In November, the same year he was admitted at the Mayo Clinic, Minnesota.

Three months after his release from the clinic, in April 1961, Hemingway was at his residence in Ketchum his wife found him holding a shotgun in the kitchen. he was admitted to the Sun Valley Hospital and later he returned to the Mayo Clinic where he received electroshock treatments. He returned home in late June and was found dead in his home in Ketchum on July 2nd. Hemingway had killed himself using his favorite shotgun.

For five years, Mary maintained that his death was an accident and only later did she ever tell the world that Hemingway had killed himself. Knowledge of his suicide led to several theories related to his mental state. One thing that was clear in all diagnosis and analysis was that Hemingway suffered from severe depression.

So how could a person who seemed so full of life and vigor suffer from depression? His works received a lot of acclamation and he travelled the world to experience different cultures and lifestyles. If you would have read about Hemingway without reading about his suicide, you may find it somewhat unbelievable to think of him suffering from depression.

This is exactly what many people suffering from depression experience. Just because they may maintain an image of being happy for the world and society doesn't always mean that a person may not be battling demons like depression and anxiety on the inside.

Depression is insidious and it may not come with warnings or signs at all. The whole process of transitioning from being a lively and happy person to being depressed may be so gradual that you may not even realize what you went through. At first the changes may be small and simple. The feeling of sadness and hopelessness becomes more prominent that other feelings in response to anything your experience in life. This automatically makes even the smallest of struggles in life appear like huge, immovable mountains that do not let you progress into living a life of joy and motivation. As depression strengthens its grip around your life, you may start feeling how could you have enjoyed anything ever. You may even begin to find it difficult to imagine how others could be so happy about life and what is missing for you to enjoy the same happiness. As small tasks look like big mountains, the ability to accomplish any goal or complete any task becomes extremely difficult. This increases the hopelessness of achieving things in life and makes you feel helpless most of the times.

You certainly want to live your life and be happy like others around you but you just don't have the solution for this problem. Even though you want to talk to others about what you are experiencing you feel your words are not enough or you are just not able to put it in words for others to understand what or how you feel. This leads to depression controlling your life rather than you having a control over all events of your life.

Depression often begins as a reaction. It is your reaction to life and everything that life brings its way. It could have started with a situation which created stress and anxiety. An inability to change this situation could lead to a denial of how things were or are. When compounded with a lack of self-care and feelings of deep injustice towards life, you may slowly find yourself encompassed with the proverbial dark cloud that follows you everywhere even when people around you seem to be carrying sunshine and happiness. Depression is all this and much more and, in most cases, we were not even able to see it coming because it tiptoes into our lives in unknowing ways.

If you are able to relate to any one of this, then knowing what you are experiencing or being able to give a name to your feelings is the first step. No one can force you to get help. You may even want to shun those who try helping you. In the early stages of depression, you still stand a chance of getting help or doing small things that can make a difference like taking a walk, talking to someone you can open up to, or even doing something that you enjoy like cooking or singing or painting. As depression turns from mild to long-lasting and deep, your feelings of hopelessness and helplessness will increase.

While most illness or health conditions have a specific set of symptoms that you may experience or which can be used for diagnosing the problem, depression is different. It does not come with a specific list of symptoms that we can reference to find out if a person suffers from depression or not. This makes it difficult for psychologists to identify the symptoms without mistaking it for other mental health problems.

When you are depressed you become highly self-critical. So even the smallest moments of achievements can be very important, and being in the presence of people who may constantly judge you can lead to further stress and anxiety when you are battling depression. Going out seems like a challenge for fear of holding a conversation or trying to fit in. Coping with depression becomes difficult not only for you but even for people who love you and mean well for you. Sometimes, when a person tries to interact with you they may feel frustrated or angry because your reactions are not what they expected. But what many of us fail to see is that depression is time-bound. When you begin to address and accept the state of depression that you are in, the time for healing begins. For some people it can be a long journey to heal yourself completely, for others it can be a fast return to a life of happiness, joy and positivity. Psychological and social factors may play crucial roles in the time it takes to overcome depression or the reason why you ever had to experience it at all. Past trauma, substance abuse, loneliness, and low self-esteem can trigger or be one of the factors of depression. While the symptoms vary largely and professional advice is very important, identifying the risk factors can be useful in understanding what could have triggered depression in you or in someone you know who is coping with it.

Loneliness is cited by researchers and psychologists as one of the biggest reasons for depression. The lack of social support can cause feelings of helplessness and as depression tightens its grip on you, you may begin to withdraw from anyone who you may be close to as well. Even though it is one of the most difficult steps to take, you should understand that loneliness will heighten the problem and look for ways in which you can overcome loneliness. Talking to a trusted friend or family member can be very helpful. This brings me to the next big risk factor of depression – relationship problems. Since a trusted social support system is very valuable for people, when your relationship turns wrong, then a person may not only end up lonely but they may not even have someone to talk to about it. In the same way, very stressful life situations like divorce, death of a loved one or the loss of a job will negatively impact mental health causing unwanted anxiety and stress which can lead to depression.

When Suman broke up with her husband after going through marriage counselling and having invested a lot of time trying to make her marriage work, she found herself become more self-critical and more stressed even about small situations in life. From maintaining a calm demeanor before her 6 year old daughter to trying hard not to turn down social events, Suman found herself being withdrawn into a darkness that she had never thought she would experience in her lifetime. Her thoughts constantly focused on how she was not a good mother or a good wife. She continuously blamed herself for a failed marriage and found herself coping with thoughts of negativity that overshadowed anything good that happened in her life. Not only did she find herself at a loss of words to describe her situation to others but she also found it difficult to interact with others.

Like Suman, there are many partners who experience undue stress and anxiety of fulfilling their role in a relationship. When we imagine a relationship we want to think of positive feelings like respect, support, trust and happiness experienced between the partners. When these feelings begin to reverse and you link more negative than positive thoughts with a relationship then you are more likely to suffer from stress and anxiety which can eventually take the form of depression. Healthy relationships are crucial for mental health and whether it is a husband and wife or a boyfriend or girlfriend, troubled or abusive relationships can become a reason for depression. Even breakups in couples can lead to the onset of depression when the partner was very attached and did not foresee a breakup.

Unmanaged pain of any kind is in fact, considered as a risk for depression. When India's coffee king V. G. Siddhartha killed himself on July, 2019, the entire country plunge into shock and remorse. As founder of the Café Coffee Day Chain, Siddhartha had established a strong coffee culture in a largely tea-drinking nation. An entire generation linked coffee to the Café Coffee Day outlets around the country. On the evening of July 29, 2019, he asked his driver to stop when they arrived before a bridge over the Nethravati River in Mangalore. The driver was asked to wait at the other end of the bridge so that Siddhartha could take a walk. But when he did not show up after more than an hour, a search began and three days later his body was found on July 31, 2019 by local fishermen. Before killing himself, Siddhartha had written a letter addressing his company board, his shareholders, and his family. The letter talked about the pressures of business losses which had become unbearable and had caused him to take this step. This is the reality of depression and how it can fetter anyone to its chains causing people to even take their lives when they are surrounded by utter hopelessness. While VG Siddhartha had a national reputation which pushed his case of depression and suicide into the limelight, there are several business owners who cope with the demons of depression. Undue losses in any business can cause a person to lose their confidence and gradually they may slip into depression which can worsen their health and their ability to rebuild whatever they have lost.

Like VG Siddhartha mentioned in his letter, "I have failed as an entrepreneur", when you are fighting depression you may see yourself as a failure as well. You may feel that nothing can be done right or you are not capable of achieving success in your life goals. But hopelessness and helplessness of such kind is only a feeling and not the truth about your life or your abilities. Depression deprives you of this clarity of thought where you begin to believe the things you feel instead of believing in your abilities and the things you have achieved in life. When you choose to see yourself as the priority and begin to focus on the achievements of your life – even the smallest ones – you will find yourself feeling better and you may even feel less anxious about life.

When the COVID-19 pandemic led to businesses pulling down their shutters forever, many jobs were lost and many business owners found themselves dealing with one of the biggest uncertainties that they may have faced. Some businesses were more resilient than others but everyone suffered losses on a large scale. This led more people to question their capabilities. With fewer job opportunities in the market, getting a new job became more difficult. For professionals who were the sole earners in their household, this became a stressful situation where they blamed themselves for not being able to do enough for their family. Business owners who did not have adequate funds to survive the extended period of slowdown had to let go of many loyal employees and this had a deep impact on the owners. Many business owners found themselves responsible for the lack of income for employees that they fired. While the news was rife with coverage of COVID-19 numbers increasing every day, we also found ourselves dealing with bigger societal problems like loneliness, and depression which began to affect a large population around the world.

Don't give up believing in yourself even when the times are hard. Because for every person who gives into depression, there is a person who is able to successfully fight and overcome depression. The fight against depression can become a long and tiring one but there is light at the end of the tunnel, there is a silver lining behind that black cloud, and there is a shore with glistening sand awaiting you after the long voyage of deep blue waters. Make yourself the priority today and never let yourself down because your assessment of yourself matters the most.

Chapter 2:

Understanding the meaning of life

The World Wars followed by the Cold War was a period of anxiety and anticipation for many individuals. Thousands of lives were lost, homes were broken, women widowed, and children orphaned. The peace treaties following the war salved the injuries inflicted on many egos and slowly helped us return to a new normality. People who lived during this period valued life because of the uncertainty of things and how death seemed to be always lurking around the corner. During this period, bravery and courage were talked about more than how we talk about these things today. War was seen as a necessity for countries to maintain their position and reputation as a powerful nation.

Between 1941 and 1945, approximately 49,000 children were evacuated from their homes in Finland to save the children from malnutrition and the hazards of war. many of these children were only preschoolers. They were placed in foster families in Sweden. Not only did they have to live through the stress of being separated from their parents, many children also had to overcome anxieties related to adapting to the new environment in their foster homes. They had to learn a new language and adopt new cultures based on the families they lived with. On their eventual return to Finland, the children once again experienced the similar stress and anxiety of readapting to the Finnish lifestyle. For them, life was extremely stressful and disconcerting in their developmental years. Studies eventually showed that females children who had evacuated Finland were highly likely to suffer from anxiety, stress, mood disorders and even bipolar disorders. Surprisingly, it was found that these mental health problems often passed on genetically to their daughters. Imagine how life could have been for a child who has no part to play in wars and was yet separated from their families, lived with foster families where they may have developed certain ties only to be torn apart and brought home again. Imagine having to go through these emotions at a time when the child's understanding of the world and life is in its formative years. Imagine what is the meaning of life for a child who experiences this?

Today, even though the thirst of becoming a political power continues to be witnessed in governments around the world, war is no longer seen as the choicest option.

The meaning of life has changed at many levels.

In a hyperconnected world where smartphone applications make it easy to connect with others, stay busy by playing games, reading books, learning a new language or pursuing a hobby, we may come to think that no one can suffer from loneliness any longer. Without the World War tearing down families, we may feel that we live in a world more safe and secure. Unlike the wives and children of soldiers who went away at war, we no longer have to constantly lead lives of anxiety and stress awaiting the return of a loved one, not knowing about their health or welfare since there was no way to communicate except letters which took weeks to arrive. Yet, studies continuously show how the number of people suffering from mental illnesses like depression continue to be on the rise.

Innovation and technology now allows us to pick up the phone and call anyone or send a message quickly when we want to talk to someone or use health applications to monitor the health of loved ones. Unlike the families who experienced the ravages of war, we live in a world that provides us with more opportunities to socialize, to live our lives without worrying about the uncertainty of death and yet the meaning of life evades many of us. We are stuck in an even lonelier place where isolation is beginning to be perceived as a normal way of life. Even though we travel more, we take fewer trips back home to our parents, relatives, families and friends. Our time is spent more on screens and less in having real conversations with people. Food is photographed more and savored less. Photos are taken more to impress and less to serve as a memory of a good occasion. So I have realized that life has lost its meaningfulness in the conundrum of social media and an online life which robs us of our real interactions with the society.

The meaning of life or the significance of your existence is often derived from the impact you have on the society and on others' life. Most of us hold a view that a person's life is more meaningful when it is dedicated towards positive outcomes for the society or for their loved ones or for the passions they pursue like art. But let us not look at life's importance from how someone else perceives us and instead hold a mirror to ourselves and find the meaning of life in the extent of happiness with which we live it. When you have lives a life where your choices and decisions bring you satisfaction then it is meaningful already.

If you find yourself caught in turmoil because of wrong decisions and poor choices, do not anchor your success on the extent to which you have been able to make others happy. Instead, you will realize that the less you find your happiness dependent on others, the more free you will feel from the chains of duty to keep other happy. This gives you the chance to explore the purpose of your life on a deeper level – a life which does not find its purpose in someone else but identifies purpose in your own goals.

I visited a sunflower field a few years ago and I returned with a bunch of them for my house. I set them up in an old milk jug and placed it on my dining table. That evening, I had a few friends visiting my home and they loved the look of the flowers. The bright yellow flowers did seem to brighten up the room and for the few days that they lasted, I loved the look of my dining area. When they started wilting, I took a few seeds and planted them in a pot. I was pleasantly surprised to see sunflower saplings rising their heads out of the soil. For the farmer growing the sunflowers in the field, the flowers provide livelihood. He sells the flowers, the seeds and even sunflower oil. For me, however, the flowers had a different purpose. I did not intend to use them for creating revenue but only for transforming the look of my home. The milk jug on the other hand had been created with a specific purpose in mind but we can eventually use them for other purposes too. In the terms of an existentialist, only existence precedes essence for the sunflower, but for the milk jug existence precedes essence when it is used as a milk jug and essence precedes existence when it is used as a vase.

You can be the sunflower or the milk jug, and no matter which one you are like, you should know this that the meaning of life is, that which you choose to give it. If you choose to give your life meaning only through your achievements or the extent to which you can keep others happy then you will find it more difficult to cope with stressful situations on your own. This is mostly because you give yourself credit to solving problems for others but you largely overlook the need for self care. Make yourself a priority instead of putting everyone else's needs before yours. When you decide to pay attention to yourself, the meaning of life becomes clearer. You have a stronger vision of your goals, your dreams and your expectations from relationships, your work and your life. With better understanding of your emotions and feelings, you will be in a position to help others and still take care of yourself too.

When you are coping with depression, this can be a crucial step to help you look at life more positively. People suffering from depression often tend to anchor their hopes on someone else. Not sure of how life has to be lived, you may find yourself in a state of disappointment where nothing seems to be good or right. But these are only feelings that you are experiencing. By gaining insight into the meaning of life or by trying to understand the purpose of your existence, you may find yourself battling with a wide range of thoughts including your relationships, your work and the society you live in. When you find yourself projecting the purpose of your life through someone else's viewpoint, take a deep breath, stop yourself and recollect your thoughts to put yourself in the center and find out what life means to you and what is the significance of your existence. Could you be the sunflower brightening up a room? Or could you be the milk jug, being the medium for the flowers to spread their cheerfulness in the atmosphere? Every time your thoughts wander too far into becoming self-critical, then stop and take the time to return to think of the things that make you happy and things you enjoy doing. The more you focus on your own happiness, the lighter you will feel about the pressure of living for others.

So what is the meaning of life for you? What is your idea of a life lived in a fulfilling manner? What kind of a life, for you, is the 'good life'?

Your answers to these questions will help you gain insight into how you want your life to be and what are your expectations from life. When you find yourself overshadowed by the darkness and gloom of depression, life loses its meaning. That's when you begin to search inside yourself for how you really wanted life to unfold. Start creating achievable goals to create your pathway towards the life you want to live. Always make sure these goals are set for successfulness. So the goals must be feasible and you must have the resources to achieve it. They should be realistic and should eventually produce an outcome which helps you measure the successfulness of your goal. For example, you dream of a quiet life in the suburbs of a city where you can enjoy time with your family without being too far from schools for children or office for you and your partner and you want to return to painting which you are very passionate about but you haven't been doing for a long time.

This is your big goal. It will take many small steps to eventually reach this goal, but you can gradually begin moving towards this big goal by starting with one thing at a time. You can start saving for a home in the suburbs or discuss the idea with your family to understand the viability of your goal. Then together you can identify how long it could take to setup a home in the suburbs or rent a place in suburbs. You may also have to start looking for areas which are not very far from schools and offices to avoid very travel time for kids or other family members. While you are doing all this, it would also be good to resume painting. It is often mentioned that one of the best ways to overcome stress is to spend time doing something you enjoy. So, if you enjoy painting then you must dedicate some time of your day or week to painting. This will also help you regain confidence and improve your moods because you are spending time doing something you enjoy. When life has a stronger purpose and this purpose resonates in your everyday actions, then you will find yourself overcoming the clenches of depression.

Every person has their own pace to come out of stress, anxiety and depression. Take your time and set your pace with awareness of the fact that it can take time to combat depression completely. There are days when you may return to periods of helplessness and feelings that your life has no meaning at all. On those days, try to talk to someone who can inspire you to not give up and who can remind you of your passions and goals in life. As they light up your path, remind yourself that hopelessness is only a feeling. Not the truth.

Chapter 3:

Meditation

How do you react when a friend goes through a difficult time like a breakup, the loss of someone close, or financial stress? Your typical responses to your friend is mostly what you yearn for when you are going through a difficult time as well. The challenge is that everyone responds differently and you may not always find the comfort and love you want in others. This is the reason why self-love and self-compassion is crucial for anyone to lead an emotionally healthy life. When you find yourself caught in crossroads of life being suffocated by anxiety and stress or having sunk into the depths of depression, self-love and self-compassion can become your tools in fighting them. An easy way to embark on a journey of self-compassion and mindfulness is to meditate.

When you are in depression, your emotional well-being is destroyed. To reconstruct it, you need to learn to look inside yourself and find out how you react to different situations. In doing so, you find out how your mind works and the emotions you experience for a given situation. With meditation you gain clarity into these thoughts and you are able to navigate through the confusion of opinions and viewpoints which are sometimes enforced on you and sometimes become a part of you through years of conditioning. As gain greater awareness into your thoughts and actions, you will begin to realize that your life and you as a person are not defined by your thoughts and emotions. This helps you find your way as an individual who can succeed at work and personal life without being pulled down by anxiety or stress.

One of the methods of meditation which has proven to be helpful for many people around the world in relieving stress and improving emotional intelligence, is mindfulness. When you practice mindfulness, you display non-judgmental awareness of the present moment. Even though this may seem like a simple thing, it requires patience and effort.

Let us first figure out how does meditation help us at all.

When you begin to meditate you will be using a meditation exercise which may involve deep breathing. As you breathe deeply, your body begins to concentrate on the exercise of breathing which automatically takes your mind off of other things that may otherwise stress you or make you anxious. If you are stressed and you begin meditating, your body gradually relaxes and your body's stress responses like the tightening of muscles stops, making way for a relaxed state.

This is the beginning of your meditation and as you relax, your mind begins to wander once again to different thoughts. But through meditation exercises, you focus your mind on the present if you are practicing mindfulness. Other meditation exercises may have different focal points like meditation for self-compassion usually requires you to focus on the emotions you experience in different situations. But no matter which kind of meditation exercise you practice, you will begin to notice that your perspective towards life changes. You start being more aware of your reactions and others' reactions to different situations. Your emotional regulation improves and this helps you manage stress more effectively.

Research and studies have shown that people who meditate and practice mindfulness over a long period of time develop higher emotional intelligence. This helps them become more aware of stress and manage stress more effectively for themselves and for others. Because meditation requires a certain amount of discipline. it is always good to go through guided meditation exercises or sessions when you are beginning with it. Once you understand how to meditate and once you are able to handle it on your own, you can start practicing meditation without assistance or guidance. Before you begin with such guided meditation sessions, you can use different stress management practices or exercises which can later be combined with your meditation exercises.

These include listening to calm music, focusing on your breath for a minute, and creating a safe go-to place in your home where you can turn to every time you feel the need to rest and reset. This special place in your house can also be used every time you have to step out of your house for a social gathering or to visit a friend and you feel stressed or anxious about going out. When you are coping with depression, social events can be difficult to attend. So before stepping out of your house, visit your corner, and close your eyes. Breathe deeply and remind yourself of your abilities, your goals in life and the happiness you want to achieve. Anchor your thoughts in moments of joy spent with loved ones and friends and use these thoughts to spark your energy in being able to step out and visit friends and families or attend a social event. At the same time, carry your headphones and make sure your favourite music or a calm music is downloaded on your phone so when you start feeling too anxious, you can always pull out your headphones and find a corner where you can return to your moment of happiness before rejoining your friends and families. It will make your outdoor or social visits easier and you may gradually find yourself more comfortable in accepting invitations for coffee or brunch with friends. If you are a student coping with the stress and anxiety of the physical, emotional and mental changes that you are experiencing, then the same steps can be used in relieving stress.

Once you begin using these small methods to improve focus and calm your nerves, full-fledged meditation can then be introduced to your daily routine helping you find your way back to self-love and self-compassion. In extreme depression, a person's body, mind and soul are connected to the same thoughts of despair and helplessness. This means any efforts that your body makes to overcome depression will often be met by contradiction from your mind and soul and if you have made up your mind to do something, your body and soul may resist it or deep within, in your soul you may feel the desire to be happy and joyful but your body and mind think that these are impossible concepts. So, the whole process of aligning these three in a way that you can move towards positivity and feeling happy can be difficult – but it is achievable. Fighting depression will require your body mind and soul to connect not just in the feelings of negativity and hopelessness but also in fostering feelings of positivity, happiness and joyfulness.

This is where meditation can be useful. It provides you with the ability to connect your body, mind and soul so you can enter a state of calm and peacefulness. At the same time, meditation also improves self-awareness and helps you manage negative emotions more effectively. Your patience and tolerance in a situation is also enhanced through meditation and your ability to handle stress is heightened. While I have spoken of mindfulness meditation and self-love meditation. There are several other types of meditation practices that can be utilized to overcome depression. The whole idea of meditation revolves around achieving calmness of mind, body and soul by emptying your mind of all thoughts, judgements, and opinions. Meditators can sit for hours focusing on their breath and not allowing any thoughts to intervene. This is known as concentration meditation. You can use a single word or mantra to repeat continuously when you practice this type of meditation. Your point of concentration can be a candle flame, counting beads strung together like a rosary, or a repetitive gong. As simple as concentration may seem, beginners find it difficult to carry it out for more than just a few minutes. This is because our mind tends to easily get carried away by different thoughts. So, you may start with meditation that lasts only for a few minutes, and gradually you will be able to increase the duration spent on your meditation exercise.

If you are a spiritual person with strong inclinations towards religion and god, then you can also benefit from spiritual meditation which requires you to spend time trying to build your connection with God through prayer to help you seek for support in overcoming depression and to gain the mental and spiritual strength that helps you move away from negative emotions and stress. Those who practice spiritual meditation usually use typical religious items like myrrh, frankincense, sandalwood and sage to heighten their experience.

A lot of people find focus to be a difficult thing when they are sitting still. If you find this to be a problem too then consider movement meditation. You can practice this in a variety of ways like through yoga, by walking in the park or the woods, gardening, or performing dance form which involves gentle forms of motion. Since this type of meditation helps you stay in action while you meditate. The movements of your body are followed by the movement of your mind as it navigates its way through your thoughts and opinions. Moving meditation requires you to focus your attention to the movement of your body. So when you are taking a walk in the park, your focus should be one how your foot touches the ground and how does it feel as your heel touches the ground before you take your next step. When you are just beginning with movement meditation, then your actions may have to be a little slower than usual so you can take the time to focus on your actions. If you are gardening, then the digging of mud and the planting of new seeds or saplings may require things to be done slowly so you can focus on the things you are doing and be present in only those movements depriving your mind of all opinions and judgements about how or how poorly you perform any of the actions you are carrying out.

When you start meditating, studies have found that you can benefit from lower blood pressure as your body and mind relaxes through the process. Since mental pressure often leads to painfulness in the muscles because of muscle tension built when you experience anxiety or stress, meditation can also solve this problem for you. These are different symptoms of depression which are either reduced or alleviated with the help of regular meditation.

Like everything else, meditation will require time before you begin to see its benefits. Remember to set measurable goals for meditation to make sure that you don't easily fall prey to judgements and despair of not enjoying visible results very quickly from meditation. It will be a slow transition, but it will help you greatly in emerging out of the darkness you constantly experience when you are depressed.

Chapter 4:

Meeting People

Every year, Rina used to visit her parents during New Year spending an entire month with them before she would return home. Her husband and daughter would also travel with her but the husband usually left early because of work commitments. She looked forward to the time she spent at home with her mother and father. Her brother and sister-in-law also used to join them for a week or at least a few days. The feeling of being with her loved ones and chatting for hours with her mother and sister-in-law was a pleasure for Rina. They would plan her trip for months before it would happen. She would think of the foods they would eat together, the places they would visit and the relatives they would meet during her visit.

This year, it was different. Rina and her husband had filed for separation. Her 8 year old daughter would be with Rina and the husband would have full visiting rights. They found that the marriage had fallen apart over the last few years and they had grown distant. Rina was a family person. She had always taken pride in the togetherness and happiness they had shared as a family. But now that they had decided to walk different paths, Rina blamed herself for not being a good partner to her husband and she was heartbroken every time her daughter would bring up questions about why daddy wouldn't come home every night. Even though the divorce was mutual and Rina knew she wouldn't want to live in a relationship where they would have to put up a display of affection for outsiders when they weren't really in love with each other any longer; the whole process was extremely stressful. Rina was not sure any longer if she wanted to visit her parents this year. She did not talk to them over the phone as often as she did earlier. To avoid questions and judgements, Rina had also avoided socializing. For a cheerful person who loved a hearty laugh and was highly social, Rina had undergone a transformation. She was living a life that she had never imagined would be hers.

Meeting people become so difficult that she started shutting out even those loved ones who truly cared for her and were worried about her. She avoided phone calls, avoided going outside as much as possible and avoided having people come over to her house. Not sure of how to cope with anxiety and stress she was experiencing with a small daughter who needed her constant love and attention, Rina ended up fighting her emotions and mental state to ensure that her daughter is not deprived of a normal life. For a long time, she mulled over the idea of placing her daughter in a boarding school. But she realized that by distancing her daughter, she would end up inflicting more pain on her mind and soul. Not only for her daughter's sake but for her own good, Rina knew she had to set things right. Having suffered from depression for over a year, having avoided her annual visit to her parents and having avoided her friends who were truly worried about her for a long time, Rina started with small steps to overcome the stress and anxiety of meeting people.

When she started taking to her mother once again, she realized how people who really loved her and cared for her were not judging her for her actions. Instead they meant well. After a long time she spoke to her mother to her heart's content. This was a big step for Rina because after a few minutes of talking to her mother, she used to quickly hang up because she was afraid her mother would bring up the divorce or a discussion of the past or an incident which would remind her of how everything was good when she was married and that she was wrong in choosing to divorce her husband. But contrary to this, her mother was more vested in knowing about her health, her food habits, about Rina's daughter and her studies. Not only was this a relief for Rina, a long and hearty conversation with her mother left Rina feel more confident about the steps she and her husband had taken to end the marriage.

She spoke to her mother regularly but she was still not sure about her friends. Sometimes, friends can be very direct and many of her friends were also her husband's friends so the risk of entering into a conversation that involves him and how he is doing after the divorce were higher. So, Rina spoke to her mother more often and started talking to her sister-in-law as well. In a few months, they started talking about Rina's visit to her parents. But this was still a sore spot for Rina because she was afraid of meeting relatives their who may be very judgmental. She discussed her fears with her parents and they decided to visit her instead. Even though Rina missed the atmosphere of her parent's home, she was glad to have her parents with her for New Year. They kept their celebrations small with only her parents, Rina and her daughter and Rina's best friend who had constantly reached out to her. But for Rina this was till a big step. From avoiding meeting anyone at all, she was starting to build her social circle once again. This time, she will be careful because she did not want to relapse into the state of depression and loneliness that she had experienced in the last few months. Rina knew that it would take time for her to completely overcome the stress and anxiety she experiences when it comes to discussing relationships, her marriage and meeting people, but she has been able to slowly move towards a happy and joyful life just like the one she always imagined.

Just like Rina, depression can cause you to avoid everyone. This may not be because you don't want help. It is mostly because you are always thinking about how people would react to your actions or how they would judge you for the things you say. Sometimes, we end up making it so big a problem in our heads that we don't realize that there are friends and family members out there who are truly vested in helping us out and not in judging us or forcing their opinion on us. But we can find this out only when we take the step of meeting people and talking to them.

When Rina started slipping into a state of depression, she did not realize what was happening. All she knew was that she was experience a life-changing event as she went through the separation with her husband. These changes weren't just in the physical absence of her husband from the house, or the physical changes that Rina experienced as she skipped meals and fought anxiety constantly. At the same time, she was mentally coping with a storm of thoughts, opinions and judgements that surrounded all her decisions. Her body and mind connected with each other in the panic and anxiety Rina experienced. Everything that she wanted to do became more difficult and even small goals looked like mountains to Rina. Getting up every morning to make breakfast for her daughter and send her daughter to school turned into a task for her because the start of each morning was the beginning of another day of stress and anxiety. Even though she looked forward to her daughter coming back from school each afternoon, after her daughter was home, Rina was worried constantly that her state of mind may have a negative effect on her daughter. Not sure if her parenting was good enough or not, Rina would often panic about how effectively she would be able to raise her daughter in the absence of a father figure. This panic crept into her body, mind and soul deepening its clenches on Rina and making it more difficult for her to fight back.

Since she mostly spent her time on her own, it became more difficult for her to break away from all of it. As she gradually opened up to talking to her mother and meeting more people, Rina was able to feed her mind and soul with the positivity that others introduced to her through their conversations. She was able to break the thread of negativity and stress which had bound her body and mind into one. This helped her introduce positive transformations slowly and steadily into life. Even small changes like waking up without feeling sad became an achievement for Rina.

You may end up going through similar experiences.

As hard as meeting people may feel in the beginning this is one step that helps you open a new perspective towards your life and everything you are going through. Although your mind may continuously make you believe that everyone will be constantly judging you, there are some people who may only offer comfort and support without judgements. These are people who really care about you and who want to help you cope through this period. So when you first begin to open yourself up to company and conversation, it is best to meet people who are very close to you and in whom you can comfortably confide. By being in the presence of someone who truly cares of your well being and emotions, you will be able to talk about your feelings and discuss what you are experiencing with fewer concerns about being judged. You will take time to fully open up to them too, but the process will be smoother when you start with people who are less likely to judge you. Avoid pushing yourself into too many stressful situations at the same time. It can take a heavier toll on your mind and this can cause you to retract into the same state of loneliness only to avoid unwanted confrontations with people. If you find yourself in the company of someone who begins to create negativity or who seems to push you further into stress and anxiety, remember to quickly pull yourself out of the conversation and leave politely. You are the priority, and if anyone tries to make you feel uncomfortable about your emotions, your feelings or in any other way, then it is alright to not meet that person.

Even in a small social circle, when you are among people who make you feel good and support you then you will feel more positive and the cloud of depression on your head will feel lighter and may even fade away. Being with the right people makes a very big difference. If you find yourself avoiding company then begin with small conversations over the phone. There is a chance that you may not have anyone to confide in at all, in cases like these, it is also okay to reach out for professional help where you can discuss your emotions and feelings with a psychiatrist who can guide you on the road to a depression-free life. Extreme depression makes any types of conversation or any confrontation or social situation difficult. Since psychiatrists have deep knowledge of the challenges you may be facing, they will be able to offer non-judgmental advice and guidance on how to overcome the problems or hurdles you face when you try to overcome depression.

Rina's story is one among thousands of stories around the world of people trying to cope with depression in different forms, stages and phases. This is what would make it even more difficult for you. With no specific set of symptoms or problems that can clearly or accurately define depression, there are fewer chances of people understanding what makes them feel so differently about things unless the feeling becomes so permanent that they find it difficult to fight it. By meeting people and returning to some form of socialization, you will be able to find yourself getting closer to the light at the end of the tunnel.

Chapter 5:

Food, and all the Difference it Makes

17 year old Sam loved eating outside. For his parents, an easy way to get him to do something was to reward him with food from his favorite food joints. These included everything from burgers and pizzas to pastas and ice-creams. Even his friends knew his love for these foods and they would often come home with a couple of burgers or pizzas when they were visiting him. Sam always found food to be the best way to overcome any anxiety or stress he was facing. He was in class 12 and soon he would be preparing for his board exams. This meant that they had to spend more time studying.

For Sam, studies weren't a challenge. He had done well in class 11 and had always been among the top 10 ranks in his class. His parents were working professionals and doting parents. If they were not working, they were always talking about Sam and his future. They valued family time and would always find a way to spend time together in the evenings once they were back home. Sam was the only child and he had been pampered with the best of things that his parents could afford. They had also set aside money for his education to make sure Sam does not find himself paying for education loans. At the same time, Sam loved his parents and always made them proud by excelling in academics. His parents had always allowed him to make his own career choices, providing sound counsel and guidance to help him with his decisions. His teachers loved Sam too. They had a lot of expectations from Sam when it came to representation in inter-school competitions, exam scores and student leadership. Sam had held up to these expectations and now he was in the final year of his school with a new road ahead. He had discussed it with his parents, his teachers and his friends and had decided to pursue humanities. While some of his teachers had asked him about his interests in engineering and computer sciences, his parents had been supportive of his choice and had even looked up colleges that would be ideal for furthering his career interests.

Having done so well in school all the time, as he went through the different college applications, the marks requirements for entrance and the college fees, he started getting overwhelmed with the idea of completing school and starting college. Sam began to feel his parents had been working so hard and they had set aside a considerable sum of money which would be used for his education. This made him feel responsible for doing well or else he would fail his parents and his teachers. In school, friends constantly talked about how he did not have anything to worry about at all and how he was going to easily ace the exams. Suddenly, the reality of the exams and the outcome of results which would eventually decide his future became too much for Sam. Every time he would sit down for studies, he would begin thinking of how hard his parents were working to make this possible for him. In order to put in more effort for his upcoming board exams, Sam decided to dedicate more time to studying and less time with his family. His only reprieve was food.

When he felt too overwhelmed with his thoughts about the upcoming exams and his future, he would grab a packet of chips or get one of his favorite foods delivered home. He also relied on coffee or carbonated drinks to keep him awake late in the night so he could complete his studies. Sometimes, in the middle of the night, he would eat a chocolate or a candy for a sugar rush that helped him stay up a little longer. Sam wanted to make sure that he did not let down his parents or his teachers. Even though his parents missed the time they would spend together with Sam, they found it equally important to give him the time he needed to study for his exams. They respected their son's dedication to studies and always praised his hard work in front of friends and families. Sam was always happy to hear their praises. But now, every time he heard his parents praise him, he also found himself being placed on a high pedestal with the responsibility to maintain his position there. Seeing his parents talk so proudly of him, coerced him to study harder.

Coincidentally, he realized that his brain was getting so worked up with the thoughts of what his parents expected from him and what his teachers and friends thought of him, that his concentration of studies began to reduce. At the same time, his dependability on comfort foods increased so much and because he was spending less time out with friends or carrying out physical activities, he also started gaining weight. The constant sugar rush he experienced from the foods he ate and the regular consumption of carbonated drinks and caffeine made him yearn for these foods even more. Sam was now studying less even though he spent a lot of time in his room trying to prepare for his exams. His concentration on studies became lesser. When the school finally closed and exams were only a few weeks away, Sam experienced a sudden breakdown which left his parents aghast. It began late in the night. He had asked his mother to order pizza from the nearby store and some ice-cream. Since he was preparing for his exams, he decided to have food in his room. After he had his food, he went back to his studies while his parents were talking in the living room. Suddenly they heard a weeping sound and rushed to Sam's room. They were shocked to find Sam sobbing softly as he sat in a corner of the room near the window. He looked out and kept on sobbing. Both his parents walked up to him and asked him what had happened. Sam was unsure of how to describe everything he was feeling. His mind was reeling with thoughts.

What am I doing here staring out of the window when I should be studying?

How am I supposed to tell them that I am not sure if I will be able to make them proud or not?

Why am I terrified that my parents have set aside money for my higher education?

His thoughts couldn't be shaped into sentences, phrases or any words. He just looked at them and sobbed even louder. As tears flowed down his cheeks, emotions that he had locked inside himself for the last few months came gushing out. Without realizing it, Sam had reached the brink of depression finding himself agonizing over everything that his friends, families and teachers said. He was stressed about the upcoming exams to the point where his anxiety got the better of his wisdom and he could no longer focus on his studies. As the exams neared and Sam cooped up in the room, everyone believed that he was working hard studying but no one realized that he was working hard trying to cope with depression. His parents who had often treated food as the reward for his achievements, had never realized that Sam had started leaning towards food as a coping mechanism. Every time he felt to anxious or stressed, he would reach out to food to help him feel better. Sam's depression wasn't diagnosed till the time he experienced this breakdown. His parents were quick to act. With the help of a psychiatrist, and by becoming more mindful of Sam's eating habits, and involving themselves more in his studies, his parents were able to help Sam overcome depression. He passed class 12 with good marks and soon took admission in a reputed college. His parents had always supported Sam and had never realized that their support and praise could lead to a sudden fear of failure. After all they had praised him all his life time and Sam had always used it as motivation to do better and achieve more. So how did the tables turn?

There were lots of factors that played a role. Sometimes, when a person realizes how their future depends on the outcome of a certain event or situation, it can be overwhelming for them. This is also the reason why, people experience pre-marriage jitters and pre-natal or post-natal depression. It is mainly because of the knowledge of how everything that you do now would set the course for your future. If you were to fail in your exams, or do poorly in certain subjects then you may not be admitted in the college of your choice. Since you may have put in a lot of hard work towards your studies, anticipation of the outcome can be very stressful. In addition to this, when you eat unhealthy foods, your body may experience an imbalance in the flow of certain hormones which can reduce your ability to fight stress and anxiety effectively. As a result you may feel continually depressed.

We will soon discuss how the production of different hormones and chemicals affect your body and moods. For now, let us look at how different food groups can create changes which impact your mental and physical health. When our body does not get the right amount of nutrients, it does not function well which causes the mood swings or emotional imbalances that we experience. Sometimes, when you are stressed or anxious, you may end up skipping meals or not paying attention to the foods you eat. This increases stress for your body, doing more harm than good. Studies are unclear when we try to find the connection between depression and food. It is not as much a cause and effect study as it is a circle where depression triggers unhealthy eating and unhealthy diets trigger depression. Let us begin by understanding what are the different unhealthy eating habits which can negatively impact our moods.

Skipping meals is unhealthy. Since your body needs energy to be active throughout the day, skipped meals rob you of that energy and vitality that help your body stay active. Without a proper meal, you may start feeling weak and drained of energy which in turn causes your mind to feel that you are incapable of completing the work you had planned for today. If you are a working professional, this means you may have troubles achieving your daily and weekly goals. As a student you may not be able to keep up with your study goals. And if you stay at home then you may end up postponing the chores you had decided to complete on that day. If this becomes regular, you may blame yourself for not achieving your goals and you may see yourself as a failure at your work or school or in your family. Had you imagined that skipped meals could make so much of a difference in your emotional well being? Probably not. Because we try to look more closely at the events that make us feel bad about ourselves when we should actually be spending time identifying solutions to restore our emotional health. So if you have been skipping meals, it is a good time to rethink this eating habit. When you don't feel like having a lot of food, eat small, healthy meals instead like a light salad, or munch on a handful of healthy nuts or sprouts to maintain your source of energy.

Another poor eating habit that you must address or avoid is the cutting out of entire food groups from your diet. Your meals should always have variety and include different food groups to make sure you get all the nutrients you need from the food you are having. Studies show mood swings can result from low levels of zinc, iron, B-vitamins, magnesium, vitamin D, and Omega 3 fatty acids. Cutting out specific food groups from your meals would mean that you are unable to benefit from the nutrients that these food groups offer for your body. As a result, your body is deprived for essential nutrients which can impact its proper functioning. Even though it does not act independently as a cause of depression, cutting out food groups can increase the risk of being more stressed or feeling low all the time. Lots of fruits and vegetables in your diet help you stay healthy and can also life up your mood. If a diet requires you to cut off specific food groups from your meals then avoid such diets and stick to less restrictive diets which follow healthy meal plans.

Lastly, an eating habit that has become a lifestyle choice for a large part of the urban population around the world is the inclusion of refined carbohydrates in their meals. Even hough we realize that high intake of processed carbohydrates can be harmful for our health, we find many of these foods to be irresistible and sometimes difficult to give up. But these foods like white breads and pastries are the reason you may end up experiencing a sudden rise and fall in your blood sugar levels leading to mood swings, irritability and low energy. Sugary foods, alcohol, sweets and biscuits are also examples of foods which can make your blood sugar rise and fall very quickly. These foods are unhealthy for any person, but if you are already struggling through a poor emotional phase or an unwanted state of mind, then these foods can act as a catalyst in enhancing stress and creating undue health problems which can increase your depression.

Researchers have not been able to identify a direct connection between food and depression but stress eating has been studied and verified as one of the responses to stress and anxiety triggers. When you find yourself coping with a stressful situation, it is possible that you may find yourself reaching out for a tub of ice-cream from the fridge or munching on bags of chips or sleeping on an empty stomach. These behaviors can quickly impact your overall healthiness and increase the risks of depression or stressfulness in your life. Now that we understand what doesn't work for us and the food habits that we should overcome, let us also look at food habits that can help us improve our mental and emotional well being.

One of the best diets for healthy living is the kind that includes lots of fresh fruits and vegetables cooked in healthy oils or in a way that does not reduce the nutrients available in the foods. Choose foods local to your area and supplement it with healthy nuts and seeds. The reason I encourage you to choose local foods is because they have a lower carbon footprint because they have traveled less and they are sourced from local farms which means you are supporting local farmers as well. Healthy eating helps you have the energy to carry out tasks that may otherwise seem difficult to perform. It keeps you physically and mentally fit which gives you the ability to cope with depression in a better way. Good food also reduces incidences of diabetes and cardiovascular health conditions and they can improve cognitive functions. A healthy diet is recommended for anyone who wants to lead a happy and healthy life. On days when you feel that you may not be up for cooking a big meal, make a fresh salad which requires you to chop a few vegetables and put them together with seasoning according to your preferences. If you've started your morning not feeling very nice, then sip on some freshly squeezed orange juice and cut a few fruits to have a fruit salad. This way you will not be putting in a lot of time in the kitchen to make breakfast and you will begin your day on a healthy note. Sometimes a good breakfast may even help in lightening up your mood. But don't healthy food thinking that you will be able to come out of depression by doing it. Instead, it good food because your body deserves the love, care and attention that you give to it when you carefully choose what you eat.

In this way, you are able to provide your mind, body and soul with the attention and energy they need to think and work positively and shake away negative thoughts. If you are unable to choose your meals properly then visit a dietician for help with meal plans. Typically, it is agreed that you will be able to get most of the nutrients you need when you eat a variety of colored fruits and vegetables. Since feeling hungry often makes a person irritable, you can choose foods that release energy slowly to help you feel full for a long time if you do not eat frequently. Some common slow release foods include pasts, rice, cereals and wholegrain bread. In addition to these foods, you must also look for foods that support a healthy gut. Your gut is often linked with the emotions you experience. When you are stressed or anxious, your gut does not function properly and this is why many people who have anxiety problems may end up suffering from digestion-related health conditions. Lots of fibre and fluids keep your gut healthy. In addition to these, fruits, vegetables, beans, pulses, yogurt and probiotics are good for your gut.

Proteins are also necessary for your body because they contain certain amino acids which are responsible for the production of chemicals in your brain that regulate your emotions. Good sources of proteins are lean meat, fish, eggs, cheese, beans, lentils, nuts and seeds, and soya products. Your brain requires fatty acids to function well. These fatty acids like omega 3 and omega 6 come from oily fish, poultry, nuts and seeds, milk, cheese and yogurt. If you have been avoiding fats completely, then you may find this to be a concern and you may have to rely on supplements to provide your body with adequate fatty acids. Lastly, healthy meals are always complimented with adequate intake of water to stay hydrated. It is healthy for your gut and helps digestion.

Since we are discussing hydration, I find a lot of people choose beverages like tea or coffee to quench their thirst instead of plain water. Some even have carbonated drinks instead of the usual water. These drinks may either have caffeine which can provide you with a sudden burst of energy that makes you feel active for a short time, but this burst of energy is quickly replaced with a feeling of anxiety and depression as your energy levels begin to drop. This is also the reason why these drinks become addictive and create a cycle of feeling energetic and feeling low. We now have a lot of decaffeinated alternatives in the market for such drinks which can help you slowly get off the caffeine addiction, but it is good to gradually switch to plain old water which is easily available wherever you go. in the beginning, making a switch from caffeinated drinks can be difficult but as you slowly move away from it, you will realize that you start experiencing fewer mood swings and you may also find yourself managing stress and anxiety more effectively.

All these dos and don'ts about food may seem overwhelming when you try to switch overnight to a healthy diet. Just like Sam, you may find yourself reaching out for comfort foods when you are in a stressful situation. As much as it is good to avoid unhealthy foods completely, every now and then, you can enjoy pizzas, burgers and chips when you maintain an overall healthy meal plan. The trick is to enjoy your food as a source of energy and not to look at it as your go-to solution for the problems you may be facing in your life. Stressful situations require a sharp mind and a healthy body for you to cope with the stress and think about ways to overcome it. Eating unhealthy foods will slow down your body and mind and detract you from successfully overcoming your problems.

If you are taking anti-depressants or any form of medication then it is ideal to consult your doctor about the foods you are allowed to eat and those that you should not. A lot of anti-depressants require you to avoid fermented, smoked, dried or cured foods. Any food undergoes changes when it is exposed to certain processes. In the above processes, foods usually get exposed to a substance called tyramine. While it is harmless otherwise, tyramine can react with certain types of anti-depressants causing health problems. Foods that include caffeine, should also be avoided when you are taking anti-depressants because they may include tyramine as well.

Now that we have looked at food and its impacts on our mental and emotional wellbeing from the point of view of Sam, a child who resorted to comfort food to overcome stress and anxiety, let us also look at food for people who may have experienced food deprivation in one way or another and how these experiences change their relationship with food even when they have overcome food deprivation.

A study evaluating the long term effects of war time famine experienced in many parts of Europe during

World War I showed that people developed eating disorders and addictions when they were exposed to war stress. Studies conducted to understand the impacts of forced dieting and consecutive weight loss also showed that these habits can trigger different psychiatric diseases like anxiety and depression. In a 2004 study published in the Journal of Nutrition Education and Behavior, of Holocaust survivors in South Florida, it was found that the survivors had difficulty in throwing away food even when it was spoiled and they regularly stored excess food displaying anxiety and stress when food was not readily available. This is mostly because of food was not easily available for the prisoners in Holocaust camps. They often suffered starvation and were served meagre foods with very low nutritive value. As a result many prisoners died in the camps because of malnutrition and others suffered health problems even after being released from the camps.

Their relationship with food is very different to Sam's. For Sam, food was always readily available and binge eating was a result of anxiety caused by other factors like studies and the thought of how much his parents were expecting him to do well. On the other hand, for the Holocaust survivors, good food was a luxury. So when they were finally released from the camps and began to lead their lives independently, in addition to other experiences at the camp, the need to have food readily available all the time became necessary for them. Discussions about starvation and hunger often found many of the survivors experiencing anxiety and stress. The survivors were also more empathetic towards people who had to go without food. Many of the survivors developed eating disorders as a result of the trauma they experienced at the camps. A lot of them coped with depression as well.

Bridget Malcolm is an Australian Model who gained popularity for her appearances in two Victoria's Secret Fashion shows. She recently opened up about her experiences as a model in a highly competitive industry where size mattered. Malcolm forced herself on diets which did not provide her with adequate energy to perform any other activities. She would go to sleep as at 8 pm because she couldn't find the energy to stay up any longer. The famed model told that it took her 10 minutes just to walk up a flight of stairs because she never had enough energy to do anything. Eventually, her eating habits made her feel completely isolated and alone and she ended up suffering from chronic anxiety. Her digestive system was ruined and she no longer felt happy about working in an industry that she loved so much. She slowly started believing that she was not good enough for the industry and that she was a terrible model. She confesses that not only had she stopped believing in herself, she wouldn't even let others reason out with her because when she was coping with all that anxiety, she found it difficult to look at herself objectively. As a result, Malcolm forced herself to eat lesser and lesser just to make sure that she did not lose her place in the industry. It took her a long time to realize that she should break away from it and visit a therapist. After realizing how her lifestyle and food habits had hampered her emotional and physical health, Malcolm began a journey of healing herself. She had been on forced diets for such a long time that her body couldn't easily accept the changes she was making to eat healthier. The journey was a slow one, but Malcolm is a stronger person today who has been able to overcome chronic anxiety even though she believes that her journey of healing continues.

Food is our main source of energy. Too much or too little of it causes an imbalance in our body and affects the overall functioning of our body and mind. To reduce stress on our body caused by food, it is ideal to choose a balanced diet which helps us gain all the necessary nutrients. If you have experienced food deprivation because of forced dieting or other reasons, then it is understandable that the thought of food not being readily available can create panic or anxiety. To avoid such situations, maintain a well-stocked pantry in your house. If you feel anxious about queueing up for food, then try to use calming music to help you overcome any anxiety while you are standing in the queue. Regularly practice relaxation techniques and meditation to become more mindful of the present and avoid crowding your thoughts with past events which can cause stress or discomfort. Since it is always good not to throw away food, if you think that you may have difficulties throwing away food even when it goes bad then try giving it away to someone who may need it like a homeless person before the food goes bad. You will also feel good about being able to provide food to a hungry person. Knowing how difficult it can be to fight hunger, this act can also help you cope with depression more effectively because as you try to bring about a change in others' lives, you are also able to feed your would with positivity and happiness.

Even though many of us know food as a basic necessity of life, it is a luxury for some and the source of comfort for others. Your eating habits make a big difference in your health and appearance. If you have been ignoring food during depression, then it is time to shift your focus once again on yourself and love yourself and take care of it. Give your body, mind and soul the kind of food that keeps them healthy and that promotes overall wellbeing. It will help you fight depression more effectively.

Chapter 6:

Exercise

Sheena struggled with depression for years. Sometimes she found herself fighting back and recovering from all the challenges that depression put on her way, but some days she did not have the energy to do anything at all. The unwanted mood swings, and the constant thoughts of being judged by others made her resentful of everything she did - so she didn't do much at all. Even though Sheena had proved herself as one of the best managers in her company, her performance in the last few months had been below average. The first time this happened, Sheena found herself a little shaken because she always put her best foot forward at work. Thinking constantly about what could have gone wrong and why her performance had slipped to levels that she could not agree with, Sheena decided to do better next month. Her team performed below expectations again and Sheena found herself answering her bosses and to other managers in the department for her and her team's performance. Never having experienced so much humiliation in her professional life, Sheena returned to her team with stricter rules about performance pushing the members to work harder and for longer hours to make sure they do well. The team members felt even more demotivated when she quickly lost her temper when she noticed even the smallest of mistakes made by anyone in her team. She started tracking daily performance and made her team work for longer hours if they did not mee the targets. Some of the team members found this to be distasteful and they complained to human resources about Sheena's attitude towards them. A few of them requested a change in the team. One of the members even resigned stating Sheena's behavior towards the team being derogatory. When Sheena was questioned about this by the HR team, it seemed to be like she had not even realized what she was doing or how she was acting.

In the few months that Sheena had performed poorly at work, she had quickly plummeted into despair because she had always dealt with success in her professional life with early promotions and an accelerated route to becoming the manager. Sheena had never encountered failure at work and now that she tasted it, she realized that it was the most bitter experience of her professional life so far. Too sad about not being able to perform well, and equally energized about doing better next month, Sheena wanted her team to work with the same passion and zeal that she felt for achieving success. If she was working late in the office, she felt that everyone in her team should work late too because performance was the only thing that mattered. But every member had engagements and commitments outside work that they had to meet as well. This meant they were not happy about having to stay late, cutting down on their personal engagements. When they were performing well Sheena had never worried much about late work, but now that performance had dipped, Sheena started scrutinizing everything. The sudden disconnect between her and her team members caused Sheena to become more hopeless and feel more helpless about how she would ever be able to regain her position as one of the best performing managers in her department. She was spending more time at work than anyone else, and yet even after three months of putting in long hours of work, Sheena was still performing poorly.

She was not married and she was not seeing anyone either. So when Sheena returned home, she was all by herself and even at home, work took precedence above everything else. Her parents lived with her brother in the USA and Sheena did not have lots of friends. She was now anxious about going to office every day and each new email made her panic as she thought of the reports that would come in. Sheena was talking less to people in the office because she just did not want to continuously discuss her team's performance. One day as she returned home and sat down with dinner on the table, Sheena opened her laptop and scrolled through all the reports trying to make sense of everything that was going on. None of it seemed right because Sheena was a person who had a history of driving poor performers to do well. She picked up the phone and called a colleague just to get her mind off the thoughts of work and how to improve performance. This was her first phone call in many months since her performance had dropped. Even though they dodged a conversation about work for quite some time, the two eventually addressed the elephant in the room by bringing up the topic about Sheena's performance. Her colleague said that they were all surprised about how things had changed for her and how they all wanted to help her with it but because she seemed so withdrawn at work, no one had felt comfortable talking to her about it. They spoke for a long time and the colleague helped Sheena see the events that had taken place in her office from a whole new perspective. Sheena had believed everyone would be annoyed that she was not performing well but her colleague helped her understand that more than annoyed everyone was concerned about her health and wellness. That putting in late hours at work was having a toll on Sheena more than she had realized. The next day, Sheena walked up to her boss and discussed how her performance had changed her outlook towards work and that she would want to take a break. Her boss agreed that taking a break would be necessary but he also explained how it was important for Sheena to reclaim her position as a good performer before she took her break. So he asked her to put her work on priority and then take a break as soon as she could achieve her targets once again. This was not what Sheena had expected. Having struggled with performance for the last few months Sheena wasn't even sure how long it would take for her to get back on track.

She had always loved her work so Sheena took a deep breath and walked out of her boss' office with one thought in mind – there was nothing as important as herself and her wellbeing – she was the priority. So she decided to place herself on a journey of self-healing where late hours of work in the office will be replaced with time given to her health and wellness. Sheena went home with the decision to wake up early every morning and begin the day with a brisk walk around the park next to her home. Then after coming home from office, she would dedicate some time to her Zumba training and start gardening once again just like she loved to do before.

By placing the focus back on herself, Sheena took responsibility for her life and began to steer it towards her goals once again. For a short time, she had allowed her work to dictate everything that she believed in. A single poor performance made her believe that she was a failure. When she tried to overcome this by working harder, everything else including her physical, emotional and mental well being took a back seat. She even treated others with apathy because she only focused on turning her reports and work targets green. This resulted in stress for her members and for herself too. After being jolted back into understanding that she was the priority, Sheena knew that nothing was more important than her health and happiness and that of others. To achieve this, she had to find a way to release the stress that she experienced at work. At the same time, Sheena also started showing higher empathy towards her team members. This worked for her. Even though, they were unable to achieve top level performance they finally found themselves back in green in the weekly reports. The progress was slow for the team to become high achievers again. Some of the members had changed and others had been redistributed. This meant that Sheena had to focus on improving team collaboration and encourage the members of her current team to perform well without feeling too pressurized about their goals.

To release the stress and anxiety that she experienced at work, Sheena started exercising. The morning walk was helpful and rejuvenating. Although it took a few weeks to adjust to her new routine, Sheena started loving her morning walks. She could hear the birds chirping in the trees and she started recognizing others who walked in the park at the same time as her. Some of them even started waving at her when they recognized her as a regular visitor at the park. A few would bring in their pets as well. Sheena would sit down on a bench after a few rounds and breathe in the fresh air. These walks made her day a lot better and she felt like she reached office feeling more energized. The first half of her day at work was more productive because she found herself feeling more active and she felt more in control of her emotions. After work, when she returned home, Sheena would change into her Zumba clothes and visit a local gym where Zumba classes were conducted. Although she had tried doing Zumba on her own at home, Sheena found that working with a group ensured that she stayed motivated to visit the gym and do Zumba. At home, she often skipped the classes when she did not feel like doing it. Training with a group had made a difference and it often helped Sheena take her thoughts off of work and concentrate on her health and fitness. As she became the priority, Sheena was more in control of her life and felt more positive about things. She realized that work was only a part of her life and not everything that her life depicted. Her professional journey had turned difficult because her personal life had been ignored to a large extent. Sheena had been able to pull herself out from reaching the brink of depression. Realization came quickly for her and it helped her become compassionate towards herself.

Her morning walks and Zumba classes were not the only thing that helped Sheena but they played a role in helping her cope with anxiety and stress during the darker periods of her life. When you exercise, you enjoy a lot of health benefits. You body is at lower risk of heart disease, diabetes and health conditions related to blood pressure. At the same time, your sleeping patterns improve significantly and when you are exercising, you begin to feel good because of the release of endorphins which are termed as feel-good hormones. Exercise also leads to the release of proteins known as neurotrophic or growth factors which help your nerve cells grow and build new connections. This improves brain functioning and helps you feel better. Some of the physical attributes or visible symptoms of depression are poor sleep patterns, low energy, changes in eating habits, aches and pains in the body caused by chronic stress and anxiety, and an unwillingness to carry out physical activities. These symptoms manifest different in people suffering from depression but once these symptoms are visible, it will be difficult for you to break these habits. Exercising may often seem like a big task that you may want to avoid completely. Unlike Sheena who had started suffering from stress and anxiety and may have been in the early stages of depression, people who are coping with extreme depression may not be able to reason like her. If you find it difficult to think about exercising, start small and start slow. Begin by walking for only five minutes in a day. Try to walk outdoors in a park or a place where you can connect with nature instead of completing your exercise on the treadmill. If walking doesn't seem like your thing then step out and do some kind of exercise which you enjoy. Whatever physical activities you carry out, it is crucial to make it sustainable. You cannot walk for a month and start feeling good only to leave it halfway through.

Exercise should be seen as a long-time treatment and it will require your dedication. On days that you don't feel like stepping out at all, try some form of exercise in the house to keep up with your routine. Avoid breaking this routine as much as possible by reminding yourself that your physical and mental wellbeing is important and that you are the priority. The key will be to choose a form of exercise that you know you will want to keep doing. When you meet your exercise goals, even small ones, you will begin to gain more confidence and feel positive about yourself. By taking your workout outdoors like at a park, a gym or a training class, you will be able to meet others and sometimes new interactions can be helpful in taking your mind off worries. It also helps you cope with depression and anxiety in a healthy way where you take positive steps to manage stress instead of dwelling over it in your mind and overthinking people's responses or opinions. There is no specific form of exercise which can be used for coping with depression. Physical activity of any kind like running, jogging, walking, swimming, gardening, washing the car, and cycling are good ways of getting your muscles to work. To make sure that exercising works for you and is able to help you overcome depression, begin by choosing something that you like. If you like to play basketball then visit a nearby basketball court or install a basket in your house and try to spend some time playing basketball. This way, you will be doing something you enjoy and you are more likely to stick to that activity. Start with small goals that make it possible for you to achieve your targets easily. Increase your goals gradually so you can spend more time exercising every week. When you are starting off, take the time to think of things that may stop you from achieving your goals. if you are likely to give up early because you prefer working with a partner then try to get a friend to exercise with you or join a gym where you can exercise with a buddy. Once you know what is stopping you from achieving your fitness goals, you can also come up with alternatives or solutions to help you achieve those goals.

If you play a sport with a team then you will end up bonding with the players and this can be very useful in allaying stress and anxiety. Thomas Plante, a professor of psychiatry and behavioral sciences at Stanford University in California said that group exercises keeps people more engaged and energized while individual exercises were more contemplative and stress reducing. The outcomes produced by both were good for anyone coping with anxiety and stress related problems.

Governments around the world have started focusing on the importance of green gyms so many parks in towns and cities have equipment to help you work out in the open while you can breathe in fresh air. This can be helpful if you prefer exercising outdoors. On the other hand if you are an indoor person then you can exercise at home or in local gyms. Remember to use exercise as a means of coping with depression and improving your overall mental and physical health. If you are on medication for depression then don't replace exercise with medication. Instead, compliment your medication with exercise after consulting with your doctor on the types of exercise which will be good for you. Your doctor will also be able to advise you if you should avoid any kind of exercise based on your medical condition.

At the same time, researchers have found that exercising should always be carried out in moderation. If you begin obsessing over exercise and undertake high-intensity workouts for longer periods of time then you may end up experiencing more stress and anxiety. If you enjoy your exercise, remember to keep it sustainable and balanced. Create a routine for your exercising to ensure you do not end up thinking of doing more, more and more. Most doctors agree that working out for 150 minutes per week is adequate for your body. According to WHO guidelines this is the minimum amount of time you should spend doing some form of physical activity in a week. It helps you prevent a lot of health problems and improves mental health too.

Chapter 7:

Rediscover Your Passion

Kavya felt like she was full of life when she sat down with her canvas on an easel and a palette in her hands. The gentle strokes of brush on the canvas transported her into the paintings she was making. During the time that she painted, Kavya forgot everything else around her. Sometimes, it was like therapy, at other times she was driven into an obsession to complete her paintings with the accuracy and beauty she imagined in her head. She would stay up late in the night working on the canvas with the least thought of the time or of others who may want her attention. Kavya was going turn 30 in a few months and her parents wanted her married. But she did not want to rush into relationships because she had been in and out of a lot of bad relationships. Every relationship started the fun ride of happiness and the feelings of excitement and undying love for each other but then came the arguments about her work hours, her hobbies and her lifestyle. Slowly, the arguments would turn into days of not talking to each other before the relationship would end. Kavya felt drained every time this happened. She wasn't sure what went wrong for her or why she was the only one who could not sustain a long-term relationship when friends around her were getting married.

She was working in the marketing department for a multinational company in Delhi. Her parents lived in a small town located a day's journey away from Delhi. Kavya visited her parents a couple of times in the year. She had a younger sister who was still studying and lived with the parents. The father held a government office and had ensured good education for both the children. Money wasn't a problem in their home and Kavya enjoyed financial independence. She did not have to send money home and her father had taught her to save right from her first paycheck. The life Kavya lived in Delhi was very different from the kind she had back in her hometown. In Delhi she led fast-paced life with little or no time for herself. When she was not working, Kavya was cleaning her home, visiting friends or shopping. Painting had taken a backseat. Her brushes and easel had been stacked away.

In her office's annual party, Kavya met a co-worker and started dating him. They seemed to have a lot in common and Kavya felt confident that it was going to work for her this time. After a few dated, Kavya started discussing marriage and he was delighted about it. The two spent more time together and soon plans of marriage became a common discussion every time they were together. They spoke to their parents and the parents spoke to each other. They got engaged and a date for marriage was fixed. Kavya was surer of it now than she had been ever before. She wanted this to work and she decided that she will make compromises if needed to enjoy a happy married life. Her professional career was on the rise too. She was offered a position in their Dubai office for the next three months. The date for marriage was set after 6 months so everyone agreed that she should take up the opportunity to work in Dubai. While she spent the day at work, Kavya spent most of her evenings browsing through online website for her wedding trousseau or she would visit a mall and shop for clothes, shoes and jewelry. She spoke to her fiancé every evening after office and they planned the wedding with equal fervor. When Kavya returned from Dubai, she took a break for a week to visit her parents and plan the wedding arrangements at home. She returned to Delhi a day early and decided to call her fiancé over for dinner. When he did not return the calls she decided to spend the time on her own reading a book and going to bed early. The next day when they met at office, he wanted to talk about marriage and thought that they should postpone the date. Kavya was confused because all this time both of them had wanted to get married as quickly as possible. One thing led to another and eventually he confessed that he had been seeing another girl when Kavya was in Dubai. It was a surprise for Kavya because she had never felt anything change in their relationship. He had always sounded the same loving person over the phone calls and video chats. They had been discussing marriage all the time and he had never even blinked an eye. So what had gone wrong?

Kavya experienced a mix of feelings that she couldn't even understand. There was rage, confusion, worry, anxiety, stress and most of all, sadness. These feelings wrapped around her so quickly and so tightly that she felt like she couldn't breathe. She had just visited her family who were so happy about her wedding and who were already making arrangements for the big day. She had shopped for bridal clothes and her wedding trousseau and bought so many things for her fiancé and his family too. Then there was the feeling of being deceived. She had never felt so heartbroken. She couldn't even complete her shift at work. She left as early as she could and as soon as she was home, Kavya broke down. She sobbed, and she howled trying to make sense of everything that he had said. Sometimes she felt like it was all just a bad dream and she would shake herself out of it but nothing worked. The wedding wasn't going to happen but she couldn't pick up the phone and tell her parents, or tell anyone at all. She did not want to talk, she did not want to go to office, she just didn't want to do anything at all. Not sure when she slept, Kavya woke up next morning and called him to talk it out and to let him know that she forgave him. She wanted to put it all behind and go ahead with the marriage. But he was not sure any longer. He had found love in someone else and he wanted to cancel the marriage. Kavya had no words. She could have compromised in a marriage where both of them were in love with each other but she couldn't force someone to marry her. She called up her parents and talked to them about it. That was the last time in many weeks that she spoke to her family. Not able to continue working in the same place as him, Kavya resigned and decided to look for a new job. But for now, all she did was stay at home avoiding all kinds of interactions with her friends and families.

She hardly ate and she hardly slept thinking continuously about all the dreams that seemed to be coming true for her. Looking at all her bridal wear thinking if she could ever think of marriage again. In just three months she would have been married and they would have been visiting Mauritius for their honeymoon. She thought so much about everything that could have been that she forgot to live. Kavya was stressed and she was coping with extreme depression. She had no one to turn to, no one who could console her and no one who she could relate her feelings to. Without work, she was living on her savings and Kavya knew she would soon have to go out for interviews again. Every day she thought tomorrow would be the day when she could start looking for jobs but the next day she would be caught in her thoughts once again spending the whole day trying to wrap her head around everything that had happened in the last few months. As her savings reduced, Kavya started to look up job portals and started sending in a few emails every day. She got a lot responses but she just didn't feel confident enough to visit an office and give her interview. On days when she did go out for an interview, she panicked and was not able to do her best in the interviews. She lost job opportunities that would have seemed really to get easy when she was working. Her confidence continued to dip and one day she came home and decided to end it all. She did not want to live any longer. But she did not want to appear as a weak person. She forgot how independently she had lived for so many years. As these thoughts crossed her mind, she got a call for a last round of interview. It was like a small streak of light in the darkness that she was living in. Kavya stopped everything that she was thinking and doing and decided to focus on this interview. She had to get it right and she had to get through. She researched about the company, the board of directors, their values, previous marketing strategies and made sure she was ready for the final interview. It worked.

She got the job. But this was one step out of the world of stress and anxiety that Kavya had unknowingly accepted as her fate. As she started working, she realigned her thoughts to her work. She started talking to her family more often too discuss work and everything related to it, but carefully avoiding discussions of the broken marriage and future prospects of marriage. Every evening she had to fight hard to avoid thoughts of her last relationship. Most evenings were spent with him and now she was all by herself in her house. She felt too lonely and too sad all the time. One weekend, to run away from her thoughts, she started deep cleaning her house and found her stash of paints, easel and canvas boards. All of a sudden, Kavya knew how to take her thoughts off of everything. She cleaned up her house, cooked herself a hot meal and sat down with her paint and brushes. It was a long time since she had felt so good. Kavya painted the whole day and she enjoyed every bit of it. Now every time Kavya felt low, she would turn to painting. It helped her heal and somehow made her feel alive again. The turmoil of thoughts in her mind didn't go away completely, but the stress and anxiety eased as she painted. Having reawakened her passion, helped Kavya fight the biggest fight in her life – it helped her cope with depression.

Sometimes, the things we are passionate about are the things that can help us rekindle our love for life and everything about it. Even though Kavya's journey to healing herself will continue and it may witness setbacks or days when Kavya feels terribly lonely and sad about her past but she now had a way of coping with the sadness and loneliness. Through painting she is often able to focus her thoughts on things she loves and the life she wants rather than on things that have happened in the past which she cannot change.

A fast-paced city life offers very less in terms of relaxation and rejuvenation. Whether you are working or studying, you will find that you have very less time to relax and indulge in activities you enjoy. If you are coping with depression, these things seem even more difficult. But having a hobby offers you a way to give time to yourself – to do things that you are passionate about. Whether you like reading a book, playing an instrument, gardening, or doing something artistic, your hobbies are an excellent distraction from stressful thoughts about work, relationships or studies. Creative activities like writing poems, knitting, crocheting, embroidery, writing music or lyrics or even designing clothes help you expand your neural connections in the brain. This is known to result in the release of dopamine which is the feel good hormone that fills you with positive emotions. You can also connect with others who share your passion by joining social groups and communities for people who pursue the same hobbies. These social relationships support your mental wellbeing and help you cope more effectively with stress or anxiety.

Kavya suffered from extreme depression and she had very little help or support from others during this period. She had shut everyone out of her life because she did not want to confront anyone about the marriage that never happened. At a time like this, it is ideal to reach out to at least someone who you trust and who you can confide in. By reaching out for help you also acknowledge the problems you are facing and are willing to take necessary steps to overcome them. In addition to talking to others, using a hobby to focus your emotions and energies into the activity you are carrying out will help you keep thoughts that cause stress and anxiety, away from your mind. But just because a hobby can help doesn't mean you pick a book and started reading even though you don't like to read at all. Make sure you choose something that you enjoy and that seems purposeful. It can be something you already know or do or you can take up something completely new that you have been wanting to explore like learning a new instrument. Even people who do not suffer from mental stress find hobbies to be useful in stimulating their creativity and making their life more meaningful. For someone who is experiencing a bas phase in their life, hobbies help in reducing the painfulness or loneliness of the journey of life. If you have less help in terms of coping with anxiety or stress, then your hobby can save you from feeling lonely and sad. At the same time some hobbies also help in expanding your social circle since you can meet new people through the hobby you pursue.

Your hobby does not require you to give it time every day. In fact the good thing about hobbies or doing things you are passionate about is that they don't require you to give a fixed amount of time to them at all. In fact your passion for these activities drive you automatically to make time for them. If in the end of the day you feel burned out then you can spend a few minutes doing what you like and then go off to sleep. Overall, if you give approximately an hour a week to your hobby then it is enough to support your mental health and wellbeing. Your hobby should never feel like you have to force yourself into carrying out the activity or else it will only add to the stress you may be experiencing instead of reducing stress and anxiety.

Psychologist Mihály Csikszentmihályi explains that a person engaged in creative activity will often find themselves in a mental state known as the 'flow'. You may have experienced it when you sit down to do something you love and you realize how you are so deeply connected with the activity you are carrying out that your mind does not even wander. In an amazing way, the activity helps you achieve a state of mindfulness which would have otherwise been difficult if you are experiencing chronic stress or anxiety. Not very surprisingly, a survey conducted by Fender showed that people who played guitar as a hobby had higher patience, increased self-confidence, better work ethic and greater persistence. Keeping in mind that following our passions, can help us learn new skills, our hobbies don't just provide us a way to block negative thoughts, they also help us improve or learn a skill.

With the help of our hobbies we can hit the reset button helping our body and mind rejuvenate after a long day or a stressful week. It doesn't matter whether your hobby involves extensive physical exercise or not, your hobby will help you emerge from the depths of despair and renew your zeal for the things you love to do and for your life.

Chapter 8:

Make Yourself the Priority

Rocky had lived a carefree life when he was young but after marriage, he had settled down to take over his father's travel business. It did not take him a lot of time to understand work at their agency and he easily gelled with the rest of the employees. His father was proud to see how Rocky helped their business flourish. He loved his wife and he was very happy in the marriage. They often went on holidays to explore new destinations which would eventually go up on their product offerings at the travel agency. Life had been very kind to them and after a year of marriage his wife was expecting too. Rocky's joy knew no bounds. Both their parents were very happy to hear the good news as well. They had a beautiful daughter. Both Rocky and his wife brought up their daughter in a warm and loving environment.

Suddenly, their business started to suffer as many new companies offering lower rates and more travel experiences began to appear. With social media, companies from different geographical locations were able to target Rocky's customers. Even though they had always offered the best of services, Rocky's agency slowly started a downhill journey that caused a lot of distress in his family. With his daughter in her early school years and his wife pregnant with their second child, Rocky wanted to make sure that his family got the best of everything. But some months, they were barely able to make ends meet as business became erratic. Customers would compare their rates with global travel agents which sometimes made it difficult for Rocky and his agency to compete. Some months, to make sure that the employees were paid and his house did not face financial difficulties, Rocky had to dip into his savings. One evening as Rocky returned home, his wife discussed finances and asked if she should start looking for a job to make sure things ran smoothly. She had always been his pillar of strength and support. Rocky's parents were equally helpful and they continuously reached out to him and his father would often talk to old customers to make sure they chose their travel agency over others. For Rocky, all the support extended by his family was helpful but it was also unsettling for him to imagine that he was not able to provide for his family. With the second child due in another 5 months, Rocky did not want his wife to be looking for jobs. Instead, he wanted to make sure he could provide for everyone and ensure a steady revenue from his existing business.

The thoughts of having to see his wife look for a job or go out to work for the whole day seemed overwhelming. Even his wife had always found happiness in staying at home and raising the kids. She had even mentioned when they were getting married that she wanted to spend her married life as a homemaker so she could look after the children, the family and pursue her own hobbies. There were times when she had shown interest in the business and had contributed her skills for their business to improve profitability and resource efficiency, but overall, she had loved being at home and taking care of everyone at home. It broke Rocky's heart to think that she would have to work again if things did not stabilize in time. He started drinking more often than before and even though he was home most of the evenings, he hardly felt the urge to spend time with the family. Instead he would just watch television till he fell asleep. Rocky wasn't sure how he could tell his family that they may no longer be able to afford the standards of living that they were used to. An evaluation of the business accounts showed that they were already too deep in business loans and revival seemed difficult. Rocky had failed. The business seemed to be doomed. If they had to pull down the shutters on their office forever, survival would become very difficult. He even started looking for jobs and applying through online portals. But Rocky had never worked before. He could not find a suitable job for himself. The entire experience was new and disturbing for Rocky. He could sustain for only another 8 to 10 months before they may have to close the business permanently. The employees were asked to leave as the business tried to cut down on costs as much as possible. Rocky and his father started talking around for potential business owners who may want to lease their store so that they can gain rent from the store after it is shut down. But the rent would not be enough to cover the expenses of maintaining the standards of living they were used to. They had already let go of the drivers and the cook at home. The family was trying hard to survive this phase.

Rocky was deeply affected by all of this. He had always seem himself as a person capable of running the travel business and doing well. In fact he had done well for almost a decade before they started facing these problems. He started smoking and drinking more than usual. It was his way of coping with the problems he had to wake up and face every day. Finances did not seem to get better and even though everyone tried hard to support, it made Rocky feel even more miserable that he was not able to provide for them. He was in depression and he did not realize this because his thoughts were only about how to make his business profitable again.

Without a clear head, Rocky was not able to achieve anything at all. He did not want to talk or discuss anything with anyone in the family any longer. He felt every time they talked the discussion would end at how to stabilize the household income. This was a discussion that he was tired of. It was a question for which he did not have an answer. His life seemed to have come to a standstill and he felt like he was answerable and responsible for everything that was happening and that he had failed as a son, a husband, a father, a leader and an entrepreneur. Waking up every day was like a punishment for Rocky. His wife couldn't see him like this so she tried hard to talk to him about business and to see if she could help but Rocky got upset whenever anything about work was being discussed.

She started checking their website and keeping an eye on the web traffic. At the same time she hired a digital marketing agency to make some changes and help them work on creating a bigger online presence. Rocky and his family had always worked with customers in their local area, with people they knew and businesses that they had been serving for a long time. They had not worked on an online presence as much. Slowly, his wife started working on their online marketing strategies and they started getting queries from different businesses who were looking for competitive rates. Some of these businesses showed interest in Rocky's product offerings. His father quickly worked with Rocky to put together suitable products for the different business queries they started receiving. Even though Rocky had seemed very unsure of how to take things forward at first, beginning to put together different products and reaching out to hotels and air carriers helped him put the focus back on his business. As simple as the solution seemed to be, Rocky realized how he had placed all his focus on getting back business with customers that they had lost instead of reaching out to new customers online. Getting up from bed every day became easier as he started handling all aspects of their work. With no employees to take care of the research and to talk to hotel managers or air carriers, Rocky had to do everything himself. His wife stayed at home and worked with the digital marketing agency to strengthen their online presence and make sure that they received a steady number of customers from the internet. As they started noticing a positive trend in sales and revenue, Rocky started seeing light at the end of the tunnel.

He had spent a lot of time ignoring his family because of the state of mind in which a failing business had placed him. With the second child due in only a few days, he knew that even though the business needed his full attention, he had to work on putting himself back on the right track. Thinking about business, his family and his responsibilities had diminished Rocky's personality to how he thought others saw him. He had to look inside, build his own reputation and create an image of himself that he would love and respect. Rocky had to become his own priority to make sure that he could take care and provide for everyone else.

During the period that his company experienced severe losses and was on the brink of shutting down, Rocky's body and mind had become connected in the feeling that there was nothing that can be done to overcome the imminent closing of his business. His focus had shifted from ideas of making the business survive to ideas of providing for his family after the business closes. With constant losses and lots of debt, he did not foresee better days for his business any longer. This was the main reason why he fell into the depths of hopelessness and despair. His body failed him, he started feeling sickly more often, and he was drinking every day. Rocky's appetite wasn't the same any longer and he had no track of the meals he was having. At the same mind, his mind was distracted with thoughts of how to survive this downhill period and how to make sure that his family did not have to lower their standards of living. Thoughts of the upcoming child, his wife's post-natal requirements, his daughter's educational expenses, and his parents' medical costs kept him awake in the night. His thoughts never spared a moment to let Rocky's mind rest and not to constantly stress him out about everything that was happening. It was as if his body and mind had connected with each other on a deep level where all he could experience was helplessness for the things happening to his family. Not even for a single moment did Rocky think of his life or what was happening to him.

Sometimes, as much as we want to put everything right for people around us, we must first look inside us and put things right for ourselves. I am not asking you to be selfish in your actions. Loving and selflessly is beautiful. What I am asking you to do, is to give yourself the same amount of love and attention that you shower on others – not to stop loving or thinking for others, but to do it for yourself too. Rocky's revival from extreme depression did not depend on his business or his wife or his family, but on himself. He had to pay attention to himself – to connect his mind and body with thoughts of positivity, self-compassion and self-love. When he starts realizing how much he has been drinking and how poorly he has been eating, and addresses these problems, he will already be on managing stress more effectively because alcohol and poor diet are triggers for stress and anxiety. Additionally, when he is not drinking, he will have the ability to make better decisions in his personal and entrepreneurial life. This can lead to better choices for his business and it is possible that he may not have to shut down his travel agency at all. His wife had already opened a pathway for the revival of the business. She had been pragmatic with her approach and built a strategy which gave hope to Rocky and his father for saving the business.

As the business started picking up pace, Rocky was back into doing the thing he was most passionate about – learning more about travel and managing his business. For Rocky, running the business was his coping mechanism to emerge from depression and slowly break away from the chains of despair. He enrolled in a course for digital marketing in order to learn more about it and to build firm foundations for his company in this new business environment. At the same time Rocky also started going on morning walks and he started taking his daughter to the nearby park every evening so that he can spend more time with his daughter. While his daughter played with her friends, he would walk around the park or complete his lessons for digital marketing. It was a break from the usual monotony of working from office. Breathing in fresh air while working on his lessons or checking new client queries on the company's website or social media pages. Even though it would take time for Rocky to completely break away from depression, his work and the progress they were making on it helped him stay focused and reduced negative thoughts. He often sat down with his wife and his father to discuss new opportunities now instead of taking all the responsibility of work himself. This way, Rocky prioritized himself and by giving himself the attention his body and mind required, he was beginning to make a difference in his life and the lives of people he loved. Having made up the mind to move forward in life with a focus on himself, he realized that by understanding self-love and self-compassion, he had opened new doors for improving personal relationships, enjoying time dedicated for himself, and enhancing his work capabilities.

When you start loving yourself, you also start learning how to love others better. This improves your relationships and your emotional intelligence. By doing things you enjoy like a hobby or dedicating time to yourself, you are also helping your mind focus on positive things as you enter the 'flow'. Your mind is less distracted with negative thoughts and you feel an enthusiasm for achieving something. Overwhelming situations, especially those that cause stress and anxiety tend to rob us of the ability to think for ourselves. We get very caught up thinking about the situation and how it would change our future, the way others behave with us and our reputation or standing in the society. While these thoughts can have a deep impact on our mind, they are only situations being created in our thoughts which distract us from giving ourselves priority in the present. Instead of looming over what can happen, we must collect our thoughts and focus on how we are treating ourselves right now.

On days when you feel that depression does not allow you to step out of the bed or to enjoy a good meal or follow your passion, remember to close your eyes and meditate to bring your thoughts into the present where your body, mind and soul are craving for self love and self compassion. By loving yourself and your body, you will automatically be able to take the decision to rise up early for a morning walk or to make your breakfast and enjoy a good meal or to do the things you enjoy. The more you show compassion towards yourself and the needs of your body and mind, the easier it will be for you to fight depression because a depressed person has not just lost hope but has lost trust in his or her own self. If I feel to broken some day to get up and go to work, I remind myself everything good about my workplace like friends who stand up for me at work, the smiles from people I know, the warm cup of coffee at the office cafeteria and a chance to finish my work goals. Knowing the things I love about work energizes me to get up and get ready to go to office. Needless to say, there are lots of things at work that I may not enjoy, like a continued reminder of meeting deadlines, co-workers who I don't get along with, and extended working hours when deadlines are not met. But by focusing on these negatives I am also giving up the chance of enjoying all the things I love about my work. So I put my thoughts on all the good things and I realize how going to work is not so bad a thing at all. When you are coping with depression, even small things like making the decision of going to work may require more effort, but these small decisions when taken correctly can help you accelerate the process of healing.

By turning the negative connection created between your body and mind into a positive one, you will have the ability to cope with depression in a better way. From being more mindful about your diet, to focusing on exercise and using your hobby to get back to things you love, you will be able to strengthen your body and soul.

You are the priority. Don't ever forget this in your life. When you start coping with depression, you would probably be learning this lesion for the first time in your life that everything else is second to yourself. When you love yourself, you have the ability to love others better and be more compassionate and empathetic towards others' experiences. Every time you make yourself the priority, you choose to lead of life gratification.

Chapter 9:

Spend Time Outdoors in Nature

After retiring from a successful career, Mr. Singh wanted to settle down into a life od quiet and happiness. He had already bought a beautiful home away from the main city. He and his wife moved into their new home soon after the retirement. He would sit down and chat with his wife about the old days and every now and then he would call up his children – two sons and a daughter – who had settled well in life and had families of their own. Every time any of the children and their families came home, Mr. Singh and his wife fussed over the grandkids, playing with them for hours, talking to the children, and having sumptuous family dinners. Every time the kids would leave, the house fell silent. His wife would return to her usual routine of waking up, overseeing the cleaning and cooking and spending time reading a book, crocheting, knitting or watching TV. For Mr. Singh life after retirement was nothing like the life he had led for as long as he could remember. When he used to work, he would get up sharp at six, read the newspaper of a cup of coffee, take a shower, and switch on the television to watch news again while he got ready and had breakfast. Then it would leave for office. The whole day at office was spent mostly between meetings, quick lunches and workplace chatter among colleagues. By the time he would return in the evening, dinner would already be ready. He would spend time watching the news or if there was a cricket match going on then he would have dinner in front of the TV before he went to bed. On the weekends, he would spend the day with close friends at a local tea stall where they would gather to talk, and share a few laughs. He would take his wife out for dinner every alternate weekend and some weekends he would ask his wife to rest and watch TV while he took over the kitchen. Mr. Singh was a great cook.

Retirement took away the certainties of life that Mr. Singh had lived by all this time. He was no longer required to get up at a certain time because there was no office. He could wake up when he wanted, watch the news if he wanted or just switch to something else on the TV. Without a specific routine, he felt out of place and even though it seemed good in the beginning, he gradually found himself with more time to spare and less work to do. For years, Mr. Singh had looked forward to his retirement and he had blown up his dream of living a quiet peaceful life so out of proportion that now when he was living the dream, he no longer found it fulfilling enough.

How was he supposed to live the rest of his life with spontaneity and uncertainty after having lived a life of surety for such a long time?

The more he thought of all the time he had from morning till evening, the more desperate he became to leave all of this behind and return to work. For all the time that he had lived before retirement, Mr. Singh did not get the chance to pursue any hobbies or passions. Even though he had thought of taking something up after retirement, he had started off slow by just taking all the extra time to rest and rejuvenate his mind and body. But after a year, having seen his kids come and leave and having to deal every now and then with a slow, quiet life where he did not have much to do, Mr. Singh started feeling sad about his life. He had nothing to worry about at all. His finances were in good position, his children were doing well and both he and his wife were happy in each other's company. But all of this was not enough for Mr. Singh. He started having negative thoughts about his retirement. He started thinking if buying a house away from the city was a good decision at all. Then he started thinking about how his wife may be coping with it. Even though she said she was happy, he felt that he may have taken her away from the city and her social life too. Driving into the main city took a lot of time and there weren't many big malls or good restaurants to go to nearby. This meant they ended up watching TV most of the time. He did not even enjoy watching TV after a few months because he couldn't connect with most of the serials his wife watched and the cricket matches weren't happening all the time. Even though he wanted to join his friends every now and then back at the tea stall, it wasn't a regular thing any longer because of the distance he had to travel. He was starting to be overwhelmed as his dream retirement turned into a life event which he no longer enjoyed. Mr. Singh started yearning more for the life he had lived all these years, he wanted back the busyness with which he did things. There were days when he would cancel a dinner with friends and sit back and relax watching a movie with his wife. Then there were days when he would stay out late till 3 am with friends and wake up with a hangover. Even though he complained about not having enough time back then, he felt that his life was much better when he was working. He was in a constant state of despair now, living only in the past, reminiscing the good times at work, with friends and the dinners with his wife. Every morning he woke up to witness the day drag from sunrise to sunset and he couldn't do much but wait for his children to come home so he could spend some good time with his grandkids or wait for an invitation from his friends in the city so he could go to the city and transport himself in time to the good days of his work life. But sometimes, when the invitation came in, he would end up thinking how his friends would talk about their lives and he may not have anything to talk about at all. So he started turning down invitations. He spent less time talking to his wife because he ended up spending more time thinking about all the things that had gone wrong with his perfect retirement plan. He seemed sad and hopeless of overcoming this situation but a visit from their neighbor changed his life.

The gated society they lived in had a few other elderly persons living. Most of them used to travel very often meeting children or visiting new places. Mr. Singh had not found any friends in the society yet. Although he did stop by and talk to a few people in the evenings when his wife coaxed him into taking a walk with her, there were hardly any people who he was able to connect with. One day, the owners of the house next to them moved in. The house had stood empty since the last family moved out a few months ago. The owners of this house were also retirees and the couple visited Mr. Singh and his wife a few days after moving in. They were very pleasant and cheerful and they looked forward to a peaceful and quiet retirement. For Mr. Singh, it was like seeing a couple start on the same journey he had began about a year ago. But his neighbor was sure that retirement would be good for him. He loved gardening and he started growing lots of flowers and vegetables in the front yard. The neighbor asked Mr. Singh if he would join him for morning walks around the locality and they could visit the nearby lake in the morning. Mr. Singh was not sure but since he had nothing else to do, he decided to give it a go. They started at 5 in the morning and walked down to the lake. The fresh morning air, the cool breeze on the lake and the beauty of the place with birds chirping around was a change for Mr. Singh. He returned feeling a lot better than he had ever done in many days. That day, he even cooked a meal for his wife and they sat down and chatted heartily after a long time. Mr. Singh told her about the lake and everything they talked about. He also asked about the kind of flowers they could grow in the front yard. He felt a sudden rush of energy as he discussed going for a walk in the morning with their neighbor once again. He looked forward to seeing the lake, the surrounding trees, plants, birds and animals. Mr. Singh felt like he would wake up with a purpose once again. He would get up, read the newspaper with a purpose since he could discuss the news with his neighbor while they walked towards the lake. Then they would sit down near the lake for a while resting, and absorbing the beauty of the place before they would start for home once again.

Mr. Singh bought a pair of binoculars and a bird watching field guide to learn more about the birds he saw around the lake. During winters, the lake would be full of migratory birds. This gave Mr. Singh and his neighbor a chance to watch birds that they had never seen before. With their field guide the two would quickly find out about the bird and when they were back home they would do their research on the internet about that bird. What started as a simple morning walk soon turned into a hobby, and nature become a healer for Mr. Singh. Watching the birds, the trees, the plants and the lake full of aquatic creatures helped Mr. Singh begin a new kind of retirement life that he began to thoroughly enjoy. Days when he would wake up feeling blue became rarer and rarer. Sometimes he did end up revisiting past memories in his mind and sometimes he still had fight his way back into the present that had so many more opportunities for him, but Mr. Singh had understood that constant thoughts of life before retirement had already caused a lot of stress and anxiety and he had to find a way to be able to take a walk down memory lane without feeling stressed or depressed about it. His wife was so happy to see him regain purpose through his nature walks, that she did not want to talk about anything that would serve as a reminder of their past. Even though they had an amazing past, it became difficult for his wife to reminisce those memories without worrying that it may trigger something that would cause Mr. Singh to feel sad or depressed again. Since he never visited a doctor or a psychologist to find out if he was suffering from clinical depression, Mr. Singh had never termed the phase he experienced as depression. He just blamed himself and all the big dreams of retirement that he had created in his mind for the way he felt.

Depression isn't often easily understood by people who experience it and the family members or friends of the person who is depressed. You may feel sad all the time on the inside but to make an effort of pleasing others you may end up wearing a smile whenever you are with friends and families. Even though every day may seem like a fight, many of your closed ones may not know about it at all. This is also possible because you may end up cutting short conversations or not talking to anyone at all. Mr. Singh did all of this and he constantly experienced sadness about his situation. When he started with the morning walks, he saw them as an unnecessary way of passing time. He wasn't sure that he would enjoy it at all, but once he returned from the walk, he felt more refreshed and renewed in spirit. Very often, when you go out for a nature walk, you would realize that your thoughts begin to focus on the beauty around you, the rustling of the leaves, the calling of birds, the hide and seek of small animals like squirrels and the loveliness of wildflowers growing erratically around the path. Nature heals in different ways. Some find it calming while others find a rush of energy as they take a nature trail. Sitting by the lake, watching small creatures, birds and plants around you and gradually seeing how everything transforms season after season helps you gain insight into life beyond the human form. If you are with a friend, you may end up discussing these insights over long conversations and if you are on your own, then nature can provide a generous pathway into your own soul for contemplation and reflection in a positive way.

A 2015 study compared the brain activity of people who walked in an urban setting and those who walked in a natural setting for 90 minutes. It was found that people walking in natural settings had lower activity in the prefrontal cortex of their brain. This area of the brain is associated with higher activity when a person enters into a cycle of repetitive thoughts which focus on negative emotions. For many people, especially men, depression is seen as a weakness and they may not want to acknowledge the state of depression they are in and they may not want to turn to medication or therapy to solve the problems they face. While extreme depression may often require professional help, if you are on the brink of depression or if you are experiencing mild depression then nature walks can be one of the best self-improvement tools.

Renowned poet Walt Whitman was 53 years old when he suffered a paralytic stroke which left him severely disabled. His slow recovery under his brother's care in New Jersey made him realize how we often forget to give credit to our small achievements in life keeping our eye only on the big wins. When he started to regain the use of his body, he started celebrating even small victories like going out everyday in the open air. One of the things that he wrote in *Specimen Days* which is a collection of his letters, reflections and journal entries is:

"After you have exhausted what there is in business, politics, conviviality, love, and so on – have found that none of these finally satisfy, or permanently wear – what remains? Nature remains; to bring out from their torpid recesses, the affinities of a man or woman with the open air, the trees, fields, the changes of seasons – the sun by day and the stars of heaven by night."

Let's take a moment for this to sink in.

Isn't it true that nature has been a constant in our lives no matter how far we go back in history? The trees, the birds and the animals have shared the planet with us since eons and they continue to be an integral part of our ecosystem. Several studies have showed that nature is important not just for survival but also for our mental health. In addition to enjoying the calmness of mind and higher focus on positive thoughts when you are in a natural setting, you may also find yourself feeling more active when you are in a natural setting. Since physical activity helps in the release of endorphins which make you feel good, nature helps you feel peaceful inside and also improves your strength and stamina since you may end up exercising more. You will feel more connected with your soul when you step out in nature. The peace and quiet of nature offers a sense of peacefulness to our minds as well. There is something about nature that makes us feel better and feel more connected with ourselves. It improves emotional health not only for you when you are in depression but even when you are leading your usual life with no problems of stress or anxiety.

Chapter 10:

Begin a Journal

Sandra was 14 years old when she had started keeping a personal diary. She loved to put her thoughts into words and write about her experiences as she entered her adolescent years. Her diary became her confidante. She wrote about boyfriends, heartbreaks, acne, friends, and best friends in her diary. It held her secrets, her thoughts and her imaginations. Each night, Sandra would carefully pen down her thoughts before she went to bed. It made it easier for her to come to terms with everything she was experiencing. After all teenage life was one of the difficult phases of life - or so she had thought. By the time Sandra graduated and started working at as a journalist, she wrote so much and so often for her work that her diary got sidelined. Eventually she forgot all about her diary.

After getting married and having a child, life became busier for Sandra. She was now in her forties with her son ready to leave home for college. Sandra and her husband had been college sweethearts. Marrying him was one of the best decisions of her life. He had supported him through her professional career ensuring marriage and motherhood did not become obstacles in the successfulness of her work life. She had full time help in the house to ensure everything was well taken care of. They enjoyed international holidays, ate at the best restaurants and always made time for the family. Life had been good for Sandra. But she was slowly beginning to loathe her work. She was not sure if she wanted to continue working any longer or not. But every time she decided to take a long leave and stay at home, she felt there was no way that she could stay at home all day with nothing to do at all, so she would return to office and start working all over again. She tried to evaluate her successfulness in life by reflecting on her professional growth, her life as a mother, as a wife and a daughter. Now that her son was in college, she was no longer left with the constant need to look after the child. This made more space and time for her husband. But her husband was busy with his own work and he gave her the same amount of time that they would spend earlier – over the weekends and during vacations. Sandra started wanting more. She felt that their relationship had grown distant over the years and with their son having left the nest, she wanted to work on her relationship with her husband once again.

She started asking him questions about work and she asked him to come home early in the evenings so they could spend more time together. Her husband did not realize what was happening. He felt that he was being doubted and that Sandra was not being understanding at all by asking her to come home early every evening. Both of them had worked their way up through their career and both enjoyed leadership positions in their companies. He explained to Sandra that it wasn't easy for him to leave office early every day. Sandra on the other hand felt that he was being unrealistic since so much of work could now be handled from home as well. They started arguing over it more often. She thought he did not want to make their relationship work while her husband only want to do the best he could to make sure that his professional and personal life were well-balanced. Sandra started feeling that she had lost her identity. She had chosen not to take up more promotions because she wanted to make more time for her family. But now she started feeling like she had made a mistake and that her family didn't need her as much.

Sandra was experiencing what many of us may call mid-life crisis. Among some people, when this period is not effectively dealt with, it may turn into depression. For Sandra, things had been pretty bad so far. She felt rejected by her family even though her husband and her son loved her a lot and had not changed their behavior towards her at all. They were still affectionate towards Sandra and while the son was in college, her husband still spent weekends with her. But Sandra wasn't seeing her life through the same lens any longer. She was now irritable, anxious and stressed all the time. Her work suffered because of this too. She wasn't at her best at work and she often seemed restless and stressed at home too. Heated arguments about relationships and love became more and more common in the house. Her husband started getting tired of these continuous arguments and so he ended up spending more time away from home than usual. This sparked more arguments and caused more stress for Sandra. She ignored her diet, her work and everything she loved to do because she was constantly thinking about her relationship with her husband. She did not want to discuss this with any of her friends or families because they all knew her husband well and they all knew how much he loved her. She felt no one would understand. This made her feel even more helpless and hopeless about her situation. She tried to focus on work to see if it would ease the problems she faced in her personal life but no matter how much she tried to concentrate, Sandra found her thoughts constantly going back to her personal relationships and she started worrying more and more about her marriage. Determined to put things right and not to fail at work, she decided to apply for a year's sabbatical.

Now that she was not working, Sandra stayed at home and tried to align her personality as a homemaker. Her husband and Sandra started the sabbatical with a vacation. Sandra felt alive once again. During the period of the vacation, she felt connected in her relationship again and she was very happy. But it was only for a week before they returned home to a new normal. Sandra cooked, baked and tried to take more interest in her husband's work-related conversations. No matter how much she tried she once again found herself back in the same depths of hopelessness. Every day her husband would leave for office in the morning and come home late in the night. She no longer argued about it. Instead, she withdrew herself into a shell of sadness and despair. Even though her husband was not doing anything out of ordinary, she felt that he was ignoring him and trying to spend less time with him. None of it was true. These were only her thoughts.

Not sure who to confide in, Sandra was at her dentist's for her regular checkup when she saw that a psychologist's clinic was right across the road and decided to make an appointment. She wasn't sure if it was needed at all. So when she walked in and told the psychologist about her recent life events, she did not realize that there was a possibility that she could be stressing over things that were only being played in her mind and not in her actual life. Among all the advice and suggestions received from the psychologist one that surprised Sandra was the suggestion to begin journaling. She thought of her teenage years spent writing in the diary and thought, *Wasn't that meant for young kids?* So she asked the psychologist *Why would a forty year old keep a diary?* The answer was that it would help her better understand things that happened in her real life and her reactions and emotions to these events.

At first Sandra wasn't sure about writing a diary again so she ignored it and decided to think of the whole event of visiting a psychologist as one of her acts of imprudence done in spontaneity and without any thought. She tried coping with her thoughts by reminding herself that it is only in her mind and that everything that she is thinking may not be true. Even thought it worked a few times, she often slipped back into the same state of despair trying to make sense of a relationship that had seemed normal only until a few months ago. So when New year came and Sandra received a few diaries from her workplace, her husband's workplace and corporate offices she had friends in, she started thinking once again about what the psychologist said. She took one of the diaries and placed it inside the drawer of her bedside table. One of the mornings when she was feeling a little better than usual, she took out the diary and decided to write in it. As a journalist, writing came naturally to Sandra. She had no difficulty putting pen to paper and pouring out her thoughts. She wrote things she had felt and imagined and she ended her writing with how she had felt better than usual on that day. It made her feel good. Sandra thought it was mostly because writing reconnected her to something that she loved to do. She had chosen journalism as a career because of her love for writing. What she did not realize was that the positive feelings that came with journaling were not just because she loved to write, but because she was able to organize her thoughts and felt more in control and more aware of what she was thinking. Sandra started realizing how she ended up overthinking things and exaggerating her own ideas or thoughts about a situation. Her first day of journaling also reminded her of her teenage days when she would guard her diary and make sure no one else read what she wrote. This time as well, she decided to carefully put the diary back in her nightstand and make sure that no one else would come across it. For the first few days she wrote regularly and she liked how writing a journal came so easily to her. She was effortlessly writing her thoughts down and she felt good to be connected to some kind of a purpose. Even though she had started journaling, she found her relationship with her son and husband grow more distant. Sandra wanted to feel like she was needed. She wanted her son to ask her opinion for things and she wanted her husband to talk more about his work, and ask her view about their future and things she cared out. Since it wasn't happening any longer she felt like her importance in the family had diminished. Sandra started writing all her despairing thoughts in the journal. It became a companion of sorts for her and she wrote all her experiences in the diary as if she wanted to talk to someone about what she is going through. Journaling became her coping mechanism.

Another thing that journaling helped Sandra remember is that she had spent a long time ignoring herself. As marriage and kids took precedence in her life, Sandra forgot her own identify. She started recognizing herself and associating her achievements with her child and her husband's achievements and their happiness. She wanted to be the best mother and the best wife. This meant Sandra had started spending more time working on the successfulness of her child and her husband. If her son did not do well at school, she felt it was because she was concentrating more at work and less on him. So she gave up a few promotions at work to focus more on her child and give him more time. Similarly when her husband did well at work and was promoted, she felt proud of him and immediately saw it as her own achievement too. For Sandra, a good wife and a good mother would always put her kids and partner before herself. With this ideology, she had, in fact, been able to build a very happy life for herself up until her child went to college and started living a life of his own. It made her feel like part of her identify had been taken away. Her identify as a mother was at stake because her son was no longer reaching out to her for every decision he took. What Sandra did not realize is that even though her responsibilities as a mother and a wife are very important, they should not end up defining the person who she was. Sandra's identity was at risk because she had put too much weightage on the relationships but had ignored her own needs. Even though she grew at work, her promotions were not as fast as they should have been because she often chose not to apply for a higher position when her son was in his formative years. Her achievements at work were hardly celebrated as much as her son's good marks, his extra-curricular activities and her husband's promotions. Sandra had comfortably put her priorities aside for her family.

She forgot that her family existed and achieved so much because of her and all the efforts that she put in for them. She forgot that without her they may not be able to celebrate as many successes as they did. She forgot that her identify was not just from them but from her achievements too. She forgot that she was the priority.

Depression can make you forget that you are important. You may think of yourself as an insignificant person who does not have value in the society or is not going to be missed if you do not accept social invitations. But this is not true at all and social invitations are not intended for you to please anyone or prove yourself to others. Instead, it should be seen as a time when you can allow yourself to indulge in the joy and happiness of the event, enjoy the food, the ambience and do it all only for yourself. Not to please others but to please yourself. You are the priority and remind yourself every day of the importance of your health, your happiness and to be compassionate towards everything you do.

When you start journaling, it is important to remember that effective journaling will help you fight depression and overcome it and not cause you to loom more over the negative thoughts your mind keeps playing in a circuit. If you write down about things that make you feel sad. Don't read them over and over again. Instead, tear that page and burn it up as a symbol of your ability to overcome these thoughts. While your journal will undoubtedly have lots of stressful thoughts written in it, always try to end on a positive note by jotting down small accomplishments of the day. Try to write down your journal every day but if you find it difficult to do this on a daily basis then do it at least three times a week. Also remember to time yourself. Usually, five to ten minutes is all you will need for journaling every day. While Sandra used it as a coping mechanism, many others have been able to use journaling as a means of becoming more aware of their thoughts. When you write down what you feel, you may realize very often that your brain may be exaggerating situations and sometimes thinking of situations in a very negative way. This awareness helps you turn your thoughts on to a more positive flow.

Effective journaling has several benefits for your mental and emotional health. There is lots of research to back the fact that when we keep a journal, we become more aware of our thoughts, our emotions and our feelings. This helps us understand triggers for stress and anxiety and enables us to manage depression and other mental illnesses more effectively. It also opens new doorways into our own emotions and state of mind. This helps us understand our own needs and requirements and makes us aware of what we may want from ourselves. Journals can also helps us picture our goals in a better way and write down the things we want to achieve in life. In doing so, we are able to see ourselves more clearly and build a stronger identity for ourselves and a deeper connection with our inner soul. With the help of journaling, a lot of people are able to make themselves the priority once again. It improves their confidence and helps them overcome their own negative thinking.

Chapter 11:

Dear Girls

Sheena was one of the best students in her class. She had done well in all her exams but she came from a family with less means. So she decided to start working right after passing 12th grade. Even though she had scored high marks and would be admitted to the best of colleges, Sheena had to choose a distance learning program for higher studies and she started working at a call centre. Her father had passed away two years ago and Sheena and her elder sister had to quickly come to terms with the fact that they would have to work to survive. While her elder sister started working only a few months after her father had passed away, Sheena promised to help her sister in providing for the family as soon as she passed high school. True to her promise, she joined work once her results were out. They had a younger sister who was still studying. Sheena and her sister took responsibility for running the household and their mother was very proud of her daughters.

Once Sheena also started earning, their family enjoyed better stability in terms of finances. In the next two years, the loans were mostly paid off and her sister would be passing high school in another year. Sheena and her elder sister wanted the younger one to continue higher studies in a good college now that they could afford it. At the same time, Sheena was able to save money and spend more on herself. She had regular appointments at the salon and shopped often. She was doing well at work too and had been promoted as a supervisor. Soon after, Sheena fell in love with a manager and started dating him. So when their office announced that Sheena, the manager and a few other co-workers would be travelling to another city for a business meeting, Sheena was happy that she would get to spend more time with the manager. On their first day at the other city, Sheena and the manager went out on a dinner date after work. He had made reservations at an impressive fine dining restaurant. They spent a great evening together and on their way back to the hotel, they even kissed in the back of the cab. Sheena had kissed him a few times before but she wanted to take things slow because she had been in a few short-lived relationships before and she did not want to end up with a broken heart again.

When they reached their hotel, he walked Sheena up to her room and asked if he could stay back and they could order dessert from the hotel kitchen. Since Sheena didn't mind spending some more time with him, she agreed. After some time, he started moving closer to Sheena and his hands reached up her thigh as he tried to kiss her again. Sheena felt uncomfortable about it, but she didn't want to stop him for fear that he may not like it. She tried to move back a bit but he seemed persistent. Not sure how to make him stop, Sheena said she wanted to use the bathroom. Inside the bathroom, she tried hard o figure a way out to ask him to leave without sounding rude or impolite. She was scared if he would be persistent and forceful then she may not have a way out at all. For Sheena, there were lots of things at stake including the experience of making love for the first time. She decided to build up the courage to ask him to leave because she wanted to sleep. At the same time, she had her sister's number on speed dial just to make sure that she could reach out to her quickly if things didn't go as expected. When Sheena walked out of the bathroom, she found him waiting for her in the bed. Although she was a little surprised with it, Sheena knew she had to ask him to leave and so she did. At first, he did not like it and Sheena could feel that an argument was imminent. Her phone was clutched in her hand ready to call her sister any time. But she tried to politely make sense of the situation telling him that work and travel had caused a lot of stress for her and she was starting to have a headache and she really needed to rest. Somehow, her lie worked and he left her saying she could reach him anytime if she needed anything or if her headache turned worse. As Sheena closed the door after him, she breathed in a sigh of relief. Even though she loved him, she had not expected to move things so quickly to the bedroom.

A lot of girls experience situations like these in their lives – some more than once. There are times when these situations can be averted easily but there are times when the man on the other side may not be as understanding. This often results in forceful sex and date rapes. When women are unprepared for situations like these, they end up suffering from a traumatic experience which can scar their lives. This is why it is very important for families to raise their boys to be respectful towards women and to ensure that men understand and acknowledge a 'no' when a woman says 'no', without taking it up on their ego and being spiteful about rejection. Men should not have to enforce their powerfulness on women by hurting them physically, mentally or emotionally. Respect for women is one of the greatest gifts a man can give to the feminine population. When women are treated lovingly and respectfully, then they are able to build warm and loving homes which in turn fosters the same philosophies. She should not be treated as a cook or a maid who is going through the monotonous routines of making your meals and washing your clothes. Instead, she should be looked up on as the creator of life and the person who binds your family together in love.

Dear girls, never remove your clothes to prove your love. Even though you go on dates, it is never okay to go to bed with someone before you commit to each other as partners for life. A boy who loves you will care for you even when you have your clothes on. He is the person who should be able to buy you your sanitary pads and not condoms. When you have a boy who can take you home instead of taking you to a hotel, you will be able to see commitment that goes beyond physical love and temporary infatuation. You will often come across boys or men who may constantly remind you of your beauty and your physical appearance in order to make you feel good and to take you to bed. But a person who is truly interested in you will talk with you about your future, how you see yourself in the years to come, your dreams, your aspirations and your passions. These are things that will define you before and after your relationship and should be acknowledged by your partner as a part of everything else that they accept when they make you their girlfriend. The same thing applies to you too. While you may have personal preferences for physical appearances, a person's behavior is more important to gauge. Look for boys who really care for you and who display higher emotional awareness. In an age when we are already vouching for equality among women and they are no longer addressed as the weaker section of the society, it is important to understand that you should never have to work around words like *adjust, compromise* and *give him what he wants*. Your identity as a woman should be respected by your partner and he should be able to treat you the same way he expects to be treated by you. If a boy feels that he can ask you undress in front of him only because you are his girlfriend then you must remind him that a physical show of love or going to bed with him is an important step in your relationship which must be saved for a time after your marriage and not before marriage. Once you are recognized as a married couple by the society bound in togetherness through your vows, then the two of you can indulge in the pleasures of marriage.

There are endless stories of women being dishonored or disrespected by men who they had expected would eventually marry them. But they were stranded halfway through marriage plans only with fake promises because the boy was only interested in sleeping with her and not in marrying her. Many women find out that their partners already have marital commitments with another person after they have had sex with him. It automatically changes everything because she realizes that she was used and not loved. This scars many women who eventually become so disillusioned about love that they feel that there is no love in the world at all. Their future relationships suffer because of the experiences they have had in their past. The scars from bad relationships based only on sex mars their entire life making them less sure of themselves and less likely to trust others.

There are times when you may find it easy to say no to sex before marriage and there are times when you may find it really difficult to say no because you feel the same attraction towards him. If you give in and later your relationship falls apart, it would only hurt more. Many women lose their confidence and stopping love themselves after a breakup. This is because they end up giving priority to their partner in the relationship and measure their success in life through the happiness and joy they bring to their partner and through the successfulness of their relationship. Once they break up, they lose their path in life and are not sure how to go ahead or what to do next.

You must always see yourself as the priority. Never depend completely on someone else to keep you happy, to love you and to show you compassion. These are emotions that you deserve from yourself. When you keep yourself happy, love yourself and show compassion to yourself, then you will understand yourself better and learn how to be kind to yourself. Never give someone else the ability to rob you of your personal identity or to see you as second priority. The love and kindness you show to yourself will help you become emotionally aware of the needs of others and be kinder towards others too.

Chapter 12:

Volunteer

Life had been uncertain for Sandy for a long time. He wanted to become a musician but his parents had never been supportive of this. They wanted him to pursue a *real career*, something that involved a stable salary and a lifestyle that allowed him to settle in one place without moving from one city to another so regularly. But Sandy had loved music since he was a small child and his decision to become a music artist was made long before he had completed school. He started learning the guitar when he was 7. He quickly picked up the chords and scales and learnt the songs very easily. His tutor was very proud of Sandy. His music took precedence and soon Sandy started spending more time with his guitar and less with his books. This transition was not taken positively by his parents. They had only agreed to guitar classes thinking of it as an extra curricular activity and not as a potential chance for building a career. Both his parents were reputed lawyers and they had wanted their son to follow their footsteps and build a sound career for himself. Sandy, however, saw things differently. He was good at studies and he never had any problems in school. He chose humanities for college and quickly landed a corporate job as an intern just after college. His parents were happy to see their son start his own professional career, but Sandy was not sure how far he could see himself treading on the monotonous pathways of a corporate life. He yearned to go back to music in some way. He had very little personal time left after work so he hardly got the time to take his guitar out and strum on the strings. Slowly, he accepted that work was important and he could only ensure a stable living out of the work that he was doing. But having given up his passion took a big tool on Sandy. He felt lost and without purpose in his life.

So when a girl came in his life to fill the void, he got purpose I life again. Because of his girlfriend, Sandy looked forward to leaving early from work, going out to restaurants and being happy once again. He finally took out his guitar again and started playing it every now and then when the two were together. Sandy was happy with her and he started loving his life again. But she found someone else and broke up with Sandy. This was a big blow for him. He became very sad and slipped into depression. For Sandy, all of a sudden, everything that he loved about life was taken away. He lost his appetite, and he lost concentration at work. He could no longer enjoy the things he did and he kept thinking of things that he may have done wrong in the relationship. Sandy blamed himself for the break up. He started believing that he had not put enough into the relationship – that he should have given her more time and been more loving towards her. He started thinking of all the arguments they had and tried to play them over and over again in his head till he started blaming himself for each one of them. Waking up every morning became difficult. He would get up and as he started going through his morning routine, he would remember how she would talk to him about waking up before the sun and doing her yoga and how she would be so full of energy all the time and how she would make her laugh. Sometimes, these memories became so painful that he would break down into tears in the middle of what he was doing. He would end up sobbing for a long time till he felt so weak and drained of energy that he could not cry any longer and then he would wrap his arms around himself to comfort himself and return to what he was doing.

Sandy had never loved someone as deeply as he had loved her. Every part of him cried out to have her back. He made endless calls and sent several messages but she had moved on in life while Sandy had could take another step forward in his life at all. He wanted everything to stand still, for the time to stop and everything to go back to as it was when she was with him. He could not accept the fact that she had left her and this denial of his break up became extremely stressful for him and caused a lot of pain to people around him who couldn't see him in such a state. At work, Sandy was no longer at his best game. He did not work with the same passion and enthusiasm as he used to. This meant that friends around him started getting promoted while Sandy got stuck in the same position. It caused more pain to him but he wasn't sure how to set things right. For him, life had lost its meaning.

One day, one of his colleagues who was now heading Corporate Social Responsibility for the company asked Sandy to join him for one of their routine visits to an orphanage that they funded. Since Sandy did not have anywhere else to be, he decided to go with his friend. At the orphanage Sandy saw things that transformed his perspective of life. Some of the children were as small as five years old while others were in their teens already. They had very limited means to live by. Most of the clothes they wore had been donated to the orphanage and every meal they had was funded by some person or organization. They were thankful for each meal because sometimes funding ran low and they may not have adequate food. With so few reasons to be happy and so much to be sad about, the orphanage was still filled with a lot of positivity. The children were happy to see Sandy and his friend and greeted them gladly. They visited the office to discuss routine information about the funds and the children's progress at school. Then the warden asked Sandy and his friend to sit in the common room where the children would like to perform for them. One of them sang, another recited a poetry, another danced and lots of others talked to them about their skills in paintings, coloring and singing. They were brimming with potential.

Sandy walked back into the office and asked if he could come to the orphanage every weekend and teach the kids music. The warden was very happy and said that the children would be delighted. The same day, he visited a shop for used musical instruments and picked up two guitars. Next weekend, Sandy visited the orphanage with the two used guitars and donated it to the orphanage. He brought his own guitar as well. Interested children had gathered in the common room where they would practice guitar for an hour. Sandy started by playing a song for them and asked how many of the kids would like to be able to play the guitar the same way. He saw lots of hands shoot up in the air. He was filled with enthusiasm to see the eager kids and suddenly Sandy realized that he had found purpose in his life once again. The two other guitars were handed to two children and it was decided that Sandy would take batches of five students. He dedicated two hours on weekends to take two sets of classes for a total of 10 students in the orphanage. Every weekend, when Sandy arrived, the kids would be ready and sitting in a circle practicing whatever was taught last week. He was very happy to see the kids do so well and show so much passion towards music. It also gave Sandy a way to get back to something that he had loved so much – music.

Being with the children and teaching them music became a therapy for Sandy. He had unknowingly fallen into the depths of depression. Even though he had tried hard, he had found it difficult to fight the symptoms. Stress and anxiety had become so common for him that everything else in his life was deeply affected by depression. His health had suffered because he did not care to have his meals in time. His work suffered and he lost so many important promotions at a time of his life when growth came easily and all his friends were getting promoted. Sandy used to feel sad, helpless and hopeless all the time after his breakup. He thought he wasn't worthy of anyone and that he did not deserve o be loved. Very few people were able to realize what was happening on the inside because Sandy never broke down before others. It was probably everything about male machismo that he had learnt and seen ever since he was a child. For Sandy, men did not cry in front of others and they certainly never let others see their weakness. This meant he had never opened up with any friends or family members about depression or the things he was experiencing. For his parents, he was only going through a difficult time which is common for anyone to experience when their partner leaves them. Even at work he had never opened up much about his breakup. Only a few friends knew and even fewer friends realized that he was not coping well with depression. His body and mind had come together in stress and anxiety to give birth to depression.

But things changed when Sandy visited the orphanage. By giving back to the society and offering some kind of support to the children at the orphanage, he went through a healing process. While he helped the children learn music, Sandy started realizing how much he had given up thinking about the things he had loved and the things he was passionate about. Even though he was volunteering and did not earn anything out of the music lessons he gave, Sandy started feeling a sense of fulfilment and he became more thankful for the chance of getting back to music. Back home, he started practicing music once again to make sure he was able to teach the students properly. At work he started being more alert of his responsibilities because his thoughts no longer revolved around his past relationship and the breakup. He was spending more time thinking about which song to teach next to the kids, how to give them a chance to showcase their talent to other people, how to hone their skills, and how to help children were finding it difficult to keep up with the lessons. He also started talking about his experiences at the orphanage with his friends and a few of them put together money to buy them another guitar. This motivated the children at the orphanage and it encouraged Sandy to keep going back and teaching the kids. One of the friends also decided to bring his keyboard and teach a few keyboard lessons at the orphanage. Sandy became more involved at the orphanage and sometimes spent more than two hours with the children discussing things other than music like things they would love to do when they grow up and places they would want to visit and the professional path they want to follow. He also started funding school for one of the kids and continued to contribute his voluntary time at the orphanage by teaching the kids music. Somedays when Sandy would make them listen to top musicians to keep the kids motivated and on other days they would learn how to play to the tunes of a local song. Sandy's involvement with the children helped him overcome one of the most difficult phases of his life. But more importantly it taught him a crucial life lesson – you must love yourself and make yourself the priority. By giving time to the kids for music, Sandy was prioritizing the things he loved and was passionate about. He started playing the guitar and he started doing small gigs at local pubs that were looking for guitar player for weeknights. Sandy did not want to be a professional guitarist any longer. He wanted to be a hobbyist and he was able to enjoy a stable income as well as stay connected with music.

Very few of us get and explore the opportunity of volunteering. We get so caught up in our lives that we don't have the time to volunteer or provide support to people who need it. But when you are coping with depression, life's meaning unfolds in different ways. When you are drowning in despair, it is difficult to focus on yourself and make yourself the priority. A lot of people just want to put an end to the feeling of stress and hopelessness by taking their lives. Volunteering brings in a new perspective to life. As a volunteer you would often realize that lots of people are carrying a heavy burden of life's problems and they still find happiness in small things. It broadens your view of life and how people find ways to adjust in the lives they lead. You learn about the hardships of life experienced by several people in the society and at the same time you learn about the importance of giving yourself priority and finding happiness in even simple things in life. Volunteering also gives you the chance to change negative thoughts or at least replace them with thoughts about your volunteer work. Your brain is able to make space for thoughts other than those that bring stress and anxiety. This way you will be thinking less about life events or things that bring back bad memories.

A word of caution for volunteering is that it is work which pays you with a sense of happiness and gratification for life. You will not be earning any money from the volunteer work you do. This means that you may not be able to find fulfilment in volunteer work that you cannot connect with. For

Sandy, music was already something he was passionate about, something that he was able to easily connect with and something that he didn't mind spending time doing. This made it easy for him to connect with the children at the orphanage using music as a medium. On the other hand if they ended up doing something that Sandy wouldn't have interest in or something that he was not passionate about then even his volunteer work would have become difficult and he may not have been able to continue with it long enough. It wouldn't have given him the same amount of satisfaction either. So volunteering is gratifying only when you volunteer for work that you can connect with. If Sandy was to connect with a non-profit organization that was working to save animals, he may not have been able to easily connect with them and enjoy the volunteer work he did because he had never had pets in his house and he was afraid of dogs and cats on the streets. As a result he may not have looked forward to his volunteering work at all and he may not have been able to find release for his negative thoughts through it.

So be sure to find a non profit organization for volunteer work of a kind that you will find fulfilling. You can take English lessons, painting lessons, music classes, singing classes, dance classes and any other kind of activity which you are passionate about. I want to remind you that through your volunteer work you will be able to reconnect with yourself and learn about things that you love and are passionate about. This is how volunteer work helps you make yourself the priority and overcome feelings of stress and depression that you may be coping with.

Chapter 13:

Let's Fix the Environment Inside Your Home

Every time Mira went shopping she would make a beeline for the home décor and home improvement section. Somehow, she did not have as much fondness for dresses and shoes as she had for beautiful home décor products. Her shopping cart would have small essentials like new bath towels, essential oils and potpourri or big buys like a piece of furniture she loved or a painting that caught her eye. All those who saw her home complimented her on how beautifully she had kept the place. Even though she had two kids, she took the time to carefully clean up after them and helped them imbibe her habits of keeping a nice and clean house. Mira had been a bright student in school and college but she never pursued a career. She got married soon after completing college and she had always been a housewife. She was not sure if she had made the right decision about it because she was in an abusive marriage. Her husband did not love her a lot and he was often verbally abusive to her. She had one son and one daughter. Both were in their early teens. For Mira, her kids meant the world to her. She could not imagine a life beyond them. They were also the reason why she had stuck through her marriage for a long time. Since Mira had never worked she did not have a means of becoming an independent parent who could take care of her children. If a divorce gets contested and custody of her children is discussed then Mira will never be able to win. So she had continued to live through a bad marriage. As her kids started growing up and were less reliant on her, Mira started feeling very lonely. With a husband who had emotionally and psychologically scarred her for life, Mira often felt that she was not good at anything at all. The only thing that kept her going was the amount of time she spent with her children. But now that they were growing up even they seemed to have a life beyond their mother and with more studies, they did not have enough time for their mother. This feeling of not being wanted at all made Mira uneasy. She was first disappointed in her children and started blaming them for not loving her back enough. Her kids were confused why she would say that because they had always loved their mother. It was only that studies, extra-curricular activities, tuitions and friends kept them very busy. As a result they no longer had the time to spend with their mother. For Mira, it was difficult to understand what was going on and any explanation given by her children felt more like a reason to stay away from her. She could no longer distinguish the truth or cope with the reality of things.

Mira started feeling very sad about everything and she started crying herself to sleep very often. Her husband was not very understanding about things either which meant she had to live through a life without love. For anyone, this could be an extremely sad situation. Earlier, her kids had acted like a balm to soothe the painfulness of a failed marriage but now even her kids seemed more distant from her. Now that she wasn't needed by her family members any longer, she lost her own importance. Since Mira had never loved herself and had always blamed herself for a failed marriage, the sudden distant attitude of her children made things even worse. The truth was that her kids loved her a lot and they didn't really want to make her feel unloved, it was just that they didn't have as much time as they did earlier. Now they had to worry more about studies and their academic performance.

Every morning Mira woke up and carried out the daily chores with a heavy feeling of sadness and despair. Once the kids went to school and her husband left for office, she would cook lunch and sit down to think about her life and how things had gone downhill for her. Soon after once the kids came home, she would serve them some food and then they would get ready for tuition and tennis classes. When they came back at night she would serve them dinner and after some studying and watching TV they would soon be in bed. All this time, Mira would be hoping that they could steal away some time to be with her but it rarely happened. On weekends, they would have friends come over to their house or visit one of their friends in the society. Then they would study or watch TV and eventually sit back and relax. Mira still used to fuss over them reminding them to have food in time, to drink more water, to complete their homework and to come home in time but there was little interaction with them other than this. In all her grief of not having a loving family life, Mira ended up ignoring her health, her ow needs and her home. It was no longer the home that she was proud of. She lost the strength to constantly clean up and decorate the house. Most of the time was spent thinking why her children didn't love her anymore and what was the purpose of her life or even having fought her way through a failing marriage only to be ignored by her children too. Since most of Mira's life had revolved around her kids and home, she had few friends. She did not feel comfortable confiding in any of her friends that her kids did not give her enough time and she did not feel wanted any longer. Every single day came and went with more stress piling up on Mira as she tried to survive through a bad marriage and the feeling of not being loved by anyone.

One day she found her daughter looking up her friends on Instagram. Mira immediately realized that social media could be a way to reconnect with her children and to at least find out what they were up to. So she set up an account for herself on Instagram. She followed both her son and daughter on it and started learning more about their friend circle and the kind of life they aspired to live. Exploring Instagram to learn more about social media became an easy way to keep her thoughts away from negativity. She saw lots of Instagram influencers and found many accounts for interior decoration. For Mira, it was like she had once again found what to do with life. As she saw more and more interior décor accounts she got more inspired to make her home beautiful too. Mira started following interior designers, architects and hashtags for beautiful homes and interior decoration. It jolted her into the reality of how much she had ignored the state of her own home. Depression had made her weak and she never felt like she had the ability to do all the cleaning and decorating that she had once loved. She decided to put things right by fixing the environment in her home and making her home beautiful once again. Since she spent most of her time in the house, Mira realized that her home had become very shabby looking and it may have had a negative impact on her thoughts too.

She took photos of her house to give herself an idea of her before and after work. Mira started with her kitchen and spent an entire day cleaning up the kitchen, removing old jars, polishing the cabinets, and reorganizing her cutlery, pots, pans, and dinnerware. By the end of the day, Mira was exhausted but this was a different kind of exhaustion and the outcome was extremely gratifying. She looked around at the kitchen after she had completed all the cleaning and Mira realized how much she had ignored the one place in her house that she spent so much time in. Her exhaustion was mostly physical because of all the work she had done unlike the mental exhaustion with which she got up and went to sleep every day. In fact, she felt lighter and less burdened by negative thoughts after she had cleaned up her kitchen. Whenever Mira had stopped and taken a break, she had taken a photo of her kitchen in the middle of the cleaning process. In the night, after everyone had gone to bed, Mira opened her Instagram account and uploaded the photos of her kitchen cleaning including before and after photos. The next day she saw quite a few people had liked her post and were interested in learning about the products she had used for the cleaning and polishing of the cabinets. Mira answered and was thrilled to start cleaning the next room. As she made breakfast that day, she even put some light music which made her feel good. After a long, long time, her day had started well. She felt so good in her kitchen that she spent longer than usual in it cooking and cleaning it up again to make sure it looked nice. Having taken away all the old jars and removed all the grease and stains from her kitchen had in some way made the place more positive for Mira. After the kids left for school and her husband went to the office, Mira wasted no time to get started with cleaning up the kids' closet. She realized how she had not done this for a long time and the whole closet looked very dirty. Many of the clothes in the closet were clothes that her children had already outgrown. She realized how less time she had been spending in creating a warm and welcoming place for herself and her family in the house. Her home had been ignored just like most other aspects of her life. But she decided that she would no longer allow her home to look so poorly maintained any longer. She sorted her children's clothes and carefully organized them in the closet removing all old clothes and setting aside a few clothes that needed repair like a missing button a small hole or a torn pocket. She also made a mental note of calling the local charity to donate clothes that her children had outgrown. In the enthusiasm of cleaning up her home once again, Mira found herself feeling more energetic and she felt more in control of everything in her life. By doing simple things like sorting out the clothes, clearing up old things and giving away the clothes to the charity made her feel that her purpose in life was beyond that of being wanted by her children. She had remembered to click before and after photos of the closet and she shared them on her Instagram account just like the kitchen photos. Lots of people from different parts of the globe commented on it and asked her about the process. The validation she received from strangers motivated her to keep going. At the same time, the positive vibes of a clean home made her feel better and less anxious. Her mind was crowded with fewer thoughts about how less her children spoke to her or needed her. Instead, they were more focused on remembering how she could decorate a living space or how to organize her closet or kitchen or simply resetting the furniture to refresh the look of a place. Her home felt different and this difference improved the way she felt too. Mira was finally more confident about herself and focused on the things that she liked to do. She baked more often and went shopping for home products more often. Even though her marriage did not get any better, she knew it couldn't get any worse either. When it came to her marriage she had already accepted her fate. It was her children who had caused more stress and anxiety in the recent years for Mira. But this also helped realize that with her children soon leaving the nest she no longer had to think about being there for them or living through an ugly marriage. Her husband had remained unloving towards her for most of their marriage. Although there were very short periods of time when he would treat with more kindness, Mira had never really felt loved and respected in their marriage. So she started thinking about life beyond marriage and how it could work for her.

She regularly posted photos of her home on Instagram and soon she enjoyed a considerable fan following. Even her children noticed that she had an amazing response on her social media posts. As she got more recognition online, she even started receiving messages from brands who asked her to work as an influencer. She didn't even think twice before taking the opportunity to get paid for promoting some products or a brand. Her first paid promotion went well and Mira was now researching information on how to take better photographs and make better videos to showcase on her Instagram account. Her children were so elated to see their mother become popular of Instagram that they even tried to pitch in with help on how to work on sponsored advertisements. One of them even spoke to a company that manages influencers and encouraged their mother to work through the agency to make sure she gets paid in time. Even though she did not ask for it, Mira realized her children had started making more time out for her to help her in this new venture that she had accidently stumbled upon. Her periods of stress and anxiety were now mostly limited to days when her husband would return in a bad mood and take it out on her. But she realized how she could turn those moments around too. She would quietly let him vent out his anger and a few days later when he would realize he had been very bad to her, she would pop in a request for a new camera or a new tripod or something she needed to make her new venture successful.

Even though I may not be able to promise you the same rate of recovery or healing from depression as Mira when you start cleaning your home, I can tell you this that the environment you live in makes a big difference in how you think and how you perceive things. A cluttered place or a home filled with memories of a past that you are trying to forget will exacerbate the feelings you are experiencing. The process of cleaning up the clutter and trashing old and painful memories, you will be able to relieve you mind of the constant negative thoughts that come across every time you see these things in your house. Clean homes are also more positive and help you feel peaceful and relaxed. when your home has good lighting, adequate sunlight and a clean space with lots of green plants, you will find more tranquility and happiness when you settle into one of the living spaces in your home. Depression often makes us forget everything about ourselves and our surroundings. We so caught in negative thoughts and a sense of sadness that we stop living in reality.

Feelings of helplessness make you weak and reduce your ability to reach out to friends and family or even connect with your inner self to love yourself more and be more aware of your needs. Everyday, your body and mind connect with each other in the feelings that you experience. When you are in depression, they connect with each other in sadness and despair, but when you decide to cope with depression and you start looking at things more positively, your body and mind connect with each other in this positivity and helps you fight the stress and anxiety you are experiencing. A peaceful environment with positive vibes helps your body and mind relax and think positively too.

Some tips to help you create a positive environment in your home and at work are to declutter all living and workspaces. The process of decluttering is helpful in removing painful memories or reducing negative energies inside your home. Start slow because you may often find the whole process to be stressful too, but the outcome or the end result of decluttering is always very satisfactory. As you do away with things you no longer need, you make space for more positivity and your home becomes less burdened by unwanted stuff which draw negativity. Homes and workplaces are two areas where you spend a lot of time. By not keeping these places clean and free of clutter, you allow negativity to take over and you may experience more stress. Once you have decluttered your home and workspace, the next step is to identify ways of getting adequate sunlight into your home. Open the windows more often and let fresh air inside your home. If you live in a densely populated city or on the main road then keep the windows open in the mornings when there is less pollution and close them again once traffic rises. Spend more time in a naturally lit place in your house. Natural light helps your body feel more energetic and improves your circadian rhythms helping you get better sleep at night and have a better appetite too.

Fixing your environment is important because your body and mind need a healthy and happy environment. By keeping your home neat and clean and ensuring that your living spaces are positive, you give your mental and physical health priority. It helps your body feel more loved and your mind and body are connected in this happiness and positivity helping you cope better with depression.

Chapter 14:

Create a Routine

I remember watching a movie where a man gets out of prison after 20 years only to realize that he so no longer cut for life outside prison and then he kills himself. He was so accustomed to a life of routine where he would have breakfast at a specific time, get limited breaks for washroom and had a specific time by which they had to complete their bathing and get ready. For 20 years he had only followed orders and lived a life that put him through a monotonous routine. You would think once he gets out of prison his life would change and he would have lots of fun not adhering to any routine at all, but in 20 years roads had changed, places and people had changed and it wasn't easy for a person who had served 20 years in prison to even make friends or get a job. When I watched the movie I thought it would be a rare scenario that some feels so upset about not having a routine and ends up killing himself. But then I saw my own grandparents and lots of other elderly people who seem to be bound by a routine that they follow unfailingly every single day unless they are sick or are bedridden. They have been doing things in the same routine for such a long time that the routine has become a habit which they can longer give up. For example getting up early or getting up before the sun rises. My grandparents always woke up before the sun rose. I remember my grandfather telling me how they were always up before the sun and all home chores were completed early and breakfast was done by 7 in the morning. My grandparents knew the importance of time and putting in more work during the day because after dark work became difficult since electricity was scarce. If the electricity went out a lot of chores could not be completed, so an early to rise and early to bed routine made sense for most people who lived before independence. Even work required many people to wake up early and arrive early at the factory, the mills or whichever place they worked in. Late night work wasn't much of a thing back then. People were usually home by 6 in the evening and they spent the evening hours with the family or with a few friends sitting around the fire. Even though we had come a long way since then and electricity was no longer a problem or waking up late did not bother anyone or even staying up late in the night watching a movie was easy, my grandparents, more or less, stuck to the routine they had followed for most of their lifetime and would always be up before the rest of the household. My grandfather would go out for a walk while my grandmother would put a chair outside in the garden and enjoy the rising sun. I hardly saw them deter from this routine and when they did, it was because they were not well.

A routine helps us set pace to the life we want to live. With the help of a routine we can give time to everything that is important in our life and take time out for ourselves too. Depression usually causes us to forget everything else and lose our purpose in life. It is difficult to make sense of what you want to do and the things you want to achieve. By adding some kind of structure to your day, you will be able to work towards certain goals and even find out patterns or figure out how well you are able to adhere to the routine you create for yourself. Don't create a very tight routine or schedule for yourself. Keep things somewhat flexible and give yourself the opportunity to make small changes to your routine when required. This will help you easily adjust to a routine and build a schedule that does not stress you out or add more anxiety. I suggest a routine where you can divide your day into five parts – early morning, late morning, early afternoon, late afternoon, evening and before bedtime. Then make columns for things you plan to do and things you actually did during that time. It is also ideal to add a column for moods to help you identify any mood swings which can be related to certain triggers that you may have experienced during this period. When you look at your day's routine, it will help you understand in a better way about things that could have gone wrong and how these things can be avoided in the future.

You will find that one of the most important parts of the day that you must have control on is your mornings. Better mornings usually make for better days. On the other hand, if you woke up in a bad mood or you don't feel like waking up and going about your morning chores, then you are likely to feel bad about the rest of your day too. So when you are beginning to set a routine, focus on your mornings and make sure that your morning routine helps you get started on a happy and positive note. Since mornings are harbingers of a new day, you may have troubles walking up in the morning and starting the day if you are in depression because every day seems to drag you through lots of anxiety and stress. This is the reason why a good morning routine is crucial for you.

If you have been living with depression for a long time, try building a morning routine that makes you feel positive. It can be something very simple but effective. For example, once you are up, take a shower, get dressed and have your tea or coffee or juice. Extreme depression may make it difficult for you to start carrying out all these tasks overnight. So start slow and begin by getting yourself into the habit of doing one of the tasks in your morning routine once you get up. If waking up and taking a shower seems too much in the beginning then start by combing your hair and getting dressed. Avoid staying in your night dress for a long time because it usually means that you are not ready to begin with your day yet. Once you are out of your night dress your body and mind are encouraged to look forward to other activities that your day entails. Gradually, you can extend the activities carried out in your morning routine to include some exercise like stretching or going for a morning walk, showering and dressing, eating a healthy breakfast, taking depression medication if you are using any of it and spending at least 15 minutes in meditation. If you work then make sure you wake up in time to carry out all these activities without feeling rushed. Follow your routine at least on the weekdays or on workdays so that you can be more productive and work with less negativity clouding up your mind. It is understandable that you may have certain days when this routine does not work well. On days like these, try to carry out some of the activities and always remember to have a good breakfast to begin your day with lots of energy. Morning are also a great time for sharpening cognitive skills and carrying out tasks of the day that require more mental or physical effort. Towards the afternoon, you may start noticing a slump in your energy. Studies show that neurotransmitters like serotonin begin to decrease around 3 pm. This means that cognition and other mental tasks will suffer when carried out at this time.

Once you have set up a good morning routine for yourself, start looking at the things you do during early and late afternoon. If you are at work during this time, try to reduce the weightage of activities to carry out in the late afternoon period. Reserve this time to go through emails and carry out tasks that require less attention or focus. If you work then your early evening will be spent wrapping up things at work so you can go home. This is when you check your reports go through your list of pending work and create the next day's list of work to be done. But if you stay at home, then early evenings are a good time to spend doing some exercise like a walk in the park or an aerobic routine inside the house before you start prepping up for dinner.

Just like your morning routine, your late night routine should be one that can help you overcome any feelings of stress and despair and encourage you to have a good night's sleep. To calm your brain and sleep more peacefully, begin your late evening routine with a warm bath, and then as you slip into your night clothes, remind yourself of all your achievements for the day. Put away your phone because it causes the brain to stay active for a longer time. The blue light emitted by your phone screen trigger higher brain activity and makes it difficult for you to sleep in time. Read a book or listen to soft music or watch a relaxing show on TV. Then turn off the lights and use soft music to help your mind relax. This will help you fall asleep quickly and more easily.

With the help of a routine, you will also be able to motivate yourself to achieve more and these small achievements will help you feel good about yourself. It increases confidence and helps you cope with depression in a better way.

Chapter 15:

Restoring Emotional Balance

It will take time to recover from depression. Some people are able to successfully fight and overcome depression within months while others suffer from it for years and sometimes even for their whole life. Those who live with depression will realize that sometimes they may feel that they have fully recovered only to relapse into depression once again. The journey of restoring emotional health is different for every person. Just like coping with depression, you will realize that your emotions may sometimes be out your control. But the more aware you become of the triggers which cause sudden changes in your emotions, the more prepared you can be to fight it.

Your emotional balance will be accomplished as a cumulative product of everything else that I have talked about in early chapters. This includes a good diet, talking to people who you can confide in, meeting new people, exercising regularly, building a routine for yourself, and doing things that you are passionate about. All of these things help you make yourself the priority. Once you start thinking more about your well being and happiness, you will become more loving and compassionate towards yourself. It is important to acknowledge these positive emotions of love and happiness that you feel for yourself.

Till the time your emotions control you, the chances of dipping into stress and anxiety are high. You may even experience unwanted mood swings and sudden emotional outbursts. But when you start taking control of your emotions, you will be able to identify triggers and identify a method to control your emotions and avoid the triggers from worsening your mental health. In the last chapter we discussed a routine and how you should add a column to your routine where you can jot down your emotions during a specific period of time and how you can reflect on reasons why you experienced the negative emotions. This helps you understand the triggers. When you know what your triggers are, use meditation to help you control yourself as you experience a surge in your emotions. We should learn to experience our feelings without being overwhelmed by them. So if you come across something that may disturb your peacefulness, then it is time to stop and reorient your thoughts in order to feed your mind and soul with positive thoughts and energies that can help you overcome the negative feelings. Sometimes, you may feel to tired and weak to be able to fight all the negative emotions, but once you start doing it, you realize that it is an accomplishment that makes you feel happier and stronger and gives you the confidence to face the negative emotions that may crowd your mind.

Our reactions to a situation define the emotions that we are experiencing and the mental state that we are in. Anything that triggers anger or stress may make us react quickly to these situation where we may end up displaying anger in a way that we may later repent or we may end up responding to stress in a way that we may not like at a later stage. But knowing control our emotions and how to create a balanced state of mind helps us respond wisely instead of react recklessly to a trigger.

Shaurya had the habit of reacting to things without thinking twice of what he was doing. If a child in the playground bumped into him while running, he would immediately push the child and if the bumping didn't injure the child, the pushing would. His parents regularly talked to him about his temper and the need to control it. As an only child, he was loved and pampered but his parents were worried about his reckless reactions which hurt other people and could even put him in harm's way. He easily got into fights and would often storm into his room shutting the door after him when his parents would try to talk about self-discipline and controlling his emotions. This led him to become more bitter and easily get upset when something bad happened.

Like Shaurya, many of us, give in easily to triggers and put all our energies in recognizing the extent of the triggers and reacting to them. But it is important to refocus our thoughts and understand what could be causing the problems and to deal with the cause and not the trigger. Only by addressing the cause and wisely handling it can be solve the problem and avoid from such triggers to recur. Focus less on the trigger and more on the reason why it causes pain and how you can address that pain.

Chapter 16:

Embrace the person you become

Depression changes a person in many ways. You end up living a life that you had never thought you would. It is like being in the depths of despair and not knowing how to get out of it. When you learn to cope with depression, you learn a lot of things that involve lifestyle changes and personality transformations. When you are able to successfully overcome depression, you will realize that you are a whole new person, different from what you may have been when you slipped into depression. The changes are mostly because you are more emotionally aware of the problems that people can face when it comes to stress and anxiety. Not only does it help you gain higher emotional intelligence, it also makes you more aware of different emotions that you experience and the triggers that can cause more stress. On a typical day before depression you may have brushed these emotions aside or just called it a bad day. But now you would be more mindful of your actions and reactions and you would also show more awareness of how other act or react to certain situations. You will also find a lot of transformation in your overall lifestyle.

With a better diet and a good exercise routine, you may have moved towards a lifestyle where you value your body's healthiness and fitness. These transformations mark your victory and these are transformations that you must embrace with all your heart. Let your body and mind know that you've moved to a better lifestyle where you are in control of your emotions, your mental and physical health, and the energies surrounding you.

The process of making yourself the priority makes you aware of yourself and your surroundings. It empowers you to choose joy and happiness for yourself in a world that may constantly overwhelm and overburden you with sorrow. At first it will require a conscious effort. You will have to continuously find your connection with your soul and even though I cannot promise that sadness will not creep in, I can tell you this, when you start building on joyfulness and happiness, the burden of sorrow in your life would be lesser. Then the sadness and despair will not be able to cut too deep into your soul and they will only leave gentle marks which will go away with the salve of happiness.

Make it a point to remind yourself each day that you are the priority and that you deserve the happiness and joys that come your way. Some days you may feel that happiness may not come to you at all, but these are only feelings and your life will open windows and doors that let in lots of sunshine and dispel the darkness. Happiness does not exist without the frustrations and sorrow that we experience from time to time. When we accept both as a law of life and look at both as a way of feeling alive and living a gratifying life, we will find ourself dealing with sadness as effectively as we deal with the happy times of our life.

Chapter 17:

Call for Help

Depression is still studied and researched widely in science because there are lots of things about depression that we are still trying to understand. For example the symptoms and the triggers for depression vary vastly among different people. Even though your environment, your relationships, your health and life situations have an impact on you, depression sometimes takes hold of people who were otherwise doing well in life and had a lot of loved ones around them. We talked about some of these situations in early chapters. Even when you have a loving partner and a good support system, you may fall prey to stress and anxiety arising from something other than relationships and eventually, even though the people around you are willing to help you, it is possible that you may shun them and distance yourself from them because of your own negative perception of everything around you. While depression is mostly a fight that you will have to fight yourself, you can get ample support from your loved ones and people who care for your health and wellness. If you find yourself in an extremely difficult position where you just don't know how to put things right or how to live through one day after another, call for help.

Make this call to a person that you can comfortably talk to. Choose someone who is less likely to judge you for the decisions you make or the explanations you give to them for the situation you are in. Very few people understand depression and its repercussions, especially those who have never been in extremely stressful situations before. Your confidante can be your partner, a parent, a sibling, a friend or any relative. If you do not feel comfortable calling someone you know to discuss what you are going through then it is advisable to consider taking an appointment with a professional psychologist who can help you cope with depression more effectively. On days when you suddenly feel too stressed or depressed you can make a quick call to your psychologist and discuss it with them. Lastly, if you think professional help may be too expensive for you, there are non profit organizations that are available on call to help you temporarily if you are experiencing a panic attack or a sudden change of thoughts that makes you feel extremely depressed causing you to consider thoughts like killing yourself.

If you have never diagnosed for depression and you are not sure if the feelings you experience is because of depression or if its is just a temporary situation of stress, then the first thing to do is to reach out to a general practitioner. Your family doctor will already have your medical history so he or she can carry out preliminary diagnosis. Alternatively, if you don't have a family doctor then consider taking an appointment with a general practitioner first and explaining everything that you are experiencing. By carrying out a thorough checkup, the general practitioner can rule out other health problems which may have similar symptoms. Additionally, the doctor may also ask if you are already on medication and check the medicines to look for possible side effects that cause the same symptoms. Once you have gone through checkups for your physical health, the doctor may refer you to a mental health care provider. The next step is to visit a psychiatrist or a psychologist to discuss what you are going through. Even though you may feel a little awkward in bringing up depression, try to discuss your feelings and the recent experiences you have had when it comes to stressful situations which make you believe that you may be suffering from depression.

This will help the doctor understand what you are going through and they will make their own observations about the way you talk or sit. You may have to go through a few tests which the doctor may consider necessary to understand your physical condition as well. If the tests were conducted a short while ago then you can bring them along with you for the doctor to analyse. Psychiatrists have specialized training and expertise to treat depression and other mental illnesses. If your psychiatrist is able to conclude that you are suffering from depression then a treatment plan will be discussed to help you heal and overcome depression. There are different types of treatment plans and medications which may be available based on how extreme the depression is for you and what your symptoms are.

Reaching out for help is important because depression thrives among people who feel helpless, hopeless and alone. The more you cut yourself out of the society and from people you love, the worse your depression would get. This is the reason why staying connected with people is very crucial when you are living with depression. If you find it difficult to socialize with many people, limit yourself to a few friends and families who understand you and whose company you are comfortable in; but always remember to have someone available who you can call for help. This help can come in the form of encouragement to achieve your goals or in the form of comfort required when you may be feeling extremely sad or hopeless. Having someone to talk to helps you vent out all your feelings and acknowledge how bad you have been feeling. As you talk about yourself and the situation you are in, you become more aware of the triggers and how you may have slipped into a very stressful situation. Talking also makes you realize that there are people out there who care about you and your wellbeing. This opens new doors for hope and makes you realize that help is available and you may only have to sometimes take the step to reach for it like making a call or sitting down with a friend to discuss the problems you have been facing.

Conclusion

A frog once looks at a single flower on a plant and asked how the flower felt in all its glory looking so splendid and having such a bright and vibrant color when everything else around it was so green and mundane. The frog said that he hated how he was just the same color as the many leaves of the plant, the moss on the roadside and the weeds in the pond. He also wanted to be different and unique like the flower that everyone appreciates and that everyone is in awe of. To this, the flower responded that it had never really felt happy about looking different. As the only flower on the plant, it stood out among the green leaves and was never able to easily meld in with the rest of the plant. Even though flower wanted to have friends, other assumed the flower to be snobbish and high-headed so they did not include the flower in any of their conversations. *To tell you the truth*, the flower said to the frog *it really very lonely to be what I am and all I ever think of is to end it all and quickly wither and die.* The frog was surprised to hear this and he said he would be happy to be friends with flower. It put a smile flower's face and they started talking, soon, a bee came to flower and joined in the conversation and not very long after, the leaves were interested in the stories of the flower, the frog and the bee. In a few days, as the flower began to wither, it said it was happy that it had the best life and the best friends and best conversations with them. In a short time, the flower had transformed from being sad and hopeless to being a happy flower that looked forward to the beginning of each day. All it needed was a gentle nudge to talk.

A lot of us, go through experiences similar to that of the flower. These experiences come from our own judgements about others and our perception about how the society will treat us. It creates mental blockades in our mind which prevent us from reaching out to people for help, socializing or holding conversations with others. When you are living with depression or other mental illnesses, these blockades become stronger and more difficult to knock down. It limits our own thoughts from crossing the line and thinking positively. Instead, we get stuck in a vicious loop of negative thoughts that cause constant stress and anxiety. Eventually, we become so overwhelmed with these thoughts that we give up hope of being able to enjoy life ever. This feeling of despair continues to tighten its grip on us till we start feeling that no one can save us from it now. As a result, helplessness creeps in making us feel that this is how life would remain forever – a dark storm of stressful emotions. These feelings are so intense that we believe them to be our reality and our body and mind get connected in this feeling of sadness and loneliness. But these are only feelings and the reality is waiting for us to make an effort to look beyond feelings of grief, despair, hopelessness and helplessness.

Fixing it is not easy but it is not impossible either. Taking control of your life will require a daily effort to carry out activities which your body and mind will think is not possible to do. Like getting up and following a daily routine, having healthy meals, exercising and meditating. Do all of this with one thing in mind, that you are the priority. In the race of life, we give everyone else so much attention and we judge ourselves based on others thoughts about us which takes away the love and compassion that we have for ourselves. Eventually we end up believing and assuming what others say about us is right and sometimes we just forget to love ourselves even when others around us have been loving and kind. Once your body, mind and soul is reminded of how much you love it and how mindful you are of your health and well being, you will automatically begin to see a positive trend in your emotional and mental health too.

Whether you are living with depression or not, promise yourself today to become your own priority. Put everything else second to your health and wellness. Practice self-love in small things like smiling at your reflection in the mirror, combing your hair, dressing up, and eating healthy foods love. Take bolder steps as you become more confident of yourself, like going out for walks, smiling at others in the park who share the same jogging or walking trail as you, taking time out for your hobbies and to do things you love. It will strengthen your perception of yourself and it will help you learn more about your feelings and your emotions. Since we mostly give credit to others for the happiness and joys in our life, we end up depending on others for all the positive feelings we experience. In depression, when we are on our own, we are unable to find a way to make ourselves feel loved and feel happy. This is where feelings of helplessness and hopelessness overpower us. But once you start loving yourself, you will be in control of your emotions and you will also know how to make yourself happy by doing things that give you joy.

Even after you are able to overcome depression, always remember that you are the priority. It will help you avoid relapses into depression and it will give you the strength and confidence to achieve your life goals and become a successful person. You may not be the same person after depression and your transformations are a sign of the positivity that you have accepted and the love you have showed to your body and mind during your healing journey. If you have already been there, you know what it is like to be depressed, so remember to offer your help and support to anyone you know who may be going through depression.

About the Author

Devesh Singh is the author behind the novel "You Are THEE PRIORITY", professionally working as an IT Project Manager with FirstRand Bank at present, an engineer by profession, a motivational speaker and has experienced his inner conscience at its peak. He has addressed the audience as a guest speaker in regards to survival of the fittest in MNC. His enthusiasm is to connect mankind to their own best being by the methods and the practices have been penned down in this book. His work across ecclesiastic disciplines broadly addresses narratives of human experience. Mr. Singh has worked in all mediums of divine and from there itself the sense was commenced of "You Are THEE PRIORITY". When you want something, the Universe conspires to help you in achieving it, he seeks to ignite this phrase into you to be the best being of you. According to the author, the beginning and end of this book make one key point: "you need to see yourself as PRIORITY, in order to see the world in its actual form. Everything in- between fuels this message, while giving you many other insights along the way". This book is a wonderful way to measure how virtuous the life you live actually is and at the very same moment a great reminder that it's never too late to struggle to get there.